BILLIONAIRE HUNT

BILLIONAIRE MATCHMAKER
BOOK TWO

SUMMER COOPER

LOVY BOOKS

PART I

1

"This sucks. This sucks so so much," Emmaline said as she and her husband Colin helped me pack up the last of the boxes. "I mean, helping you pack isn't what sucks. I mean it does, but what I'm trying to say---"

"Not very eloquently--" Colin said with a smile.

Emmaline rolled her eyes at Colin and tried again. "What I'm trying to say, if a certain someone is done interrupting, is that this whole situation sucks. I'm sorry you're going through this, Misha. I know how hard you worked to build all of this..." Her voice trailed off and she looked around forlornly at all the boxes in front of us.

I wanted to agree, but I was too busy feeling sorry for myself as I glanced around the now empty office that had once held six full-time employees. It had been a vibrant dynamic space filled with innovation and laughter. I had thought I was building an empire, but it had quickly crumbled. Designs by Misha had officially closed.

I shook my head. "I just can't believe this is happening. I worked so hard and now it's all over." My voice sounded wistful and I didn't know how much longer I could stand being in my former office without crying. And I wasn't a crier, but Emmaline had summed it up perfectly--this sucked.

"Hey, it's going to be alright. I wish I had kept my stupid mouth shut," Emmaline said, rubbing me on the back.

"Me too," I joked, taking a deep breath.

"Are you okay?"

I nodded and took another deep, shaky breath. "Just sad, that's all. This place meant a lot to me."

"I know," Emmaline said, looking just as wistful as I had moments ago, "but you'll make a comeback."

She was a lot more positive than I was. I wasn't accepting defeat in the long run, but in the short run, I had definitely failed and a comeback didn't look like it would happen anytime soon. I wasn't going to say that to Emmaline though. When we had been in college together, our other friend Lacey and I had been the ones pushing her to finish her degree. We had been Emmaline's personal cheerleaders when her life took an unexpected turn and she'd experienced an unplanned pregnancy. Being a college student and a single mom had been hard on Emmaline, but we had pushed her to keep striving anyway. And now, over 10 years later, she was returning the favor. I was used to being the strong one in my social circle. I wasn't going to let something as inconsequential as my entire career ending break me. At least, that's what I was telling myself.

"You and Colin can head out. There's nothing left. I think I can handle it from here."

"You sure?" she asked, hesitating.

I gave her a small smile. "Yes, I'm sure. And I know you have to go pick up Dora soon, so I understand if you need to head out." Theodora, or Dora as we called her, was Emmaline's preteen daughter.

Emmaline hesitantly gave me a hug. "Well, call us if you need anything and I mean anything. You know I'm a professional counselor...almost licensed...in case, you want to talk."

I gave her a half smile. "Thanks...but probably no, thanks."

She nodded. "Well, if you find yourself sitting in your closet crying...call me."

I watched them get in the car and leave, and I took one last look at the office that had been like a second home to me. I remembered how excited I had been to open this place. My husband was rarely home so I had thrown myself into my career, hoping that one day it would grow into something that rivaled his. He was an engineer and owned his own firm. The idea of being an entrepreneur intrigued me and design had always been a hobby of mine. We were well-off, but I had wanted to maintain an income and hadn't wanted to be completely reliant on Wyatt, my husband.

For five years, it had been like a dream. I had been so happy and then the local economy started to slowly unravel. My clients just dried up and I was left with nothing. I had even stopped taking a paycheck to be able to pay out something to my employees, but I knew that wasn't a sustainable solution. Finally, I let go of the dream. I'd never forget the day I called them into the conference room and told them that our company was coming to an end.

No one was surprised, but there were tears and some of those tears had been mine.

I added the last of the boxes to the trunk of my car and then locked the door of my former office for the final time.

"I'll miss you," I whispered to the building, looking fondly at the old warehouse turned lofts. With a sigh, I turned away and walked to my car.

I slid behind the wheel and my phone rang immediately. I answered it, using the Bluetooth in the car.

"Hey, girl, I'm fine," I said, expecting it to be Emmaline or my other best friend Lacey checking on me.

"Misha?"

I laughed. It was my husband. "Hi, I didn't look before answering. I just assumed you were one of the girls."

"Not a problem," he said sounding distracted. "Did you finish packing everything up?"

"Yep, just have to return the key," I chirped, trying to keep the mood light even though I didn't have a reason to.

"Sounds good. I'm sure you'll have plenty of time to take care of that tomorrow. Why don't you head on home?"

His words annoyed me. He always thought I had an infinite amount of time. But I was determined not to pick a fight over just a few questionable words.

"Are you close to home?

"About ten minutes away," I responded. "Why?"

"No reason. I'll see you soon."

He hung up then and I frowned, thinking of how his tone had been furtive, almost nervous. I hadn't heard his voice like that since he had planned a surprise birthday party for me last year.

I groaned to myself. I hoped Emmaline and Lacey hadn't convinced him to throw me a "Feel better" party or whatever they thought to call it.

Exactly ten minutes later, I pulled up into the driveway of our modern, sleek home. I loved this home, but not the price tag. I had thought it a waste of money, but Wyatt had said it was the perfect place for a CEO and his family to live. I much preferred the craftsman styled bungalows that could be found in most of the neighborhoods, but they hadn't been grand enough for Wyatt.

We were opposite in many ways. I was artistic and creative. He was a procedural guy, who saw most things in black and white; yet we'd been married for eight years, having only dated for three months before falling for each other.

As I got out of the car, I prepared myself for another crazy surprise party. I put the key in the lock, turned it and peeked in. I didn't see anyone, but the lights were low.

I stepped fully in and called out, "Wyatt? I'm home..."

"I'm in the living room," he called back.

Smiling, I made my way there to see him.

To my surprise, no one was hanging around the corner ready to yell "Surprise!"

"Hey, what are you doing in here? I thought you would be in your workshop."

He had a workshop in the back of the house where he tested new products and ideas. He could stay there for hours, only coming out to eat. Now he did most of his testing at work, but still tinkered in his workshop during late afternoons.

"Hi, why don't you sit down?" he said as he sat on the couch, drinking something that I was sure was an alcoholic beverage. Wyatt drinking during the daytime? Something was wrong.

"You okay?" I asked. I suddenly had no desire to sit down. Whatever the news was, I would just have to take it standing up.

He shook his head, not making eye contact with me even though I was directly in front of him.

"What's wrong?" I asked again.

Finally, he looked at me and his eyes were wary, but I saw resolve there. "I can't be with you anymore."

I felt as if I had been kicked in the gut, but maybe Wyatt was just being funny...but Wyatt didn't have a sense of humor.

I shook my head and said, "That's not funny, Wyatt...so if that's your idea of funny, you've failed miserably."

He didn't immediately respond. Instead he took another drink and said, "We're very different people."

"What does that even mean? And what does that have to do with anything?" I was confused, hurt and felt that my whole world was falling apart. I didn't even recognize my life anymore. I had lost my business and now Wyatt wanted to leave me? I felt as if my insides were slowly being torn out. My head was now pounding and the only thing I could think of was that I desperately needed to wake up from whatever terrible nightmare I was having.

"Wake up, Misha. Wake up...wake up," I repeated over and over. I felt ridiculous, but it was worth a shot.

"You're not asleep," Wyatt said with a sigh. "You should have seen this coming. Even I knew this was coming."

And just like that my confusion and hurt turned to anger. "I should have seen this coming? What exactly should I have seen coming, Wyatt? My husband leaving me? My husband, who promised me forever, just up and deciding that forever was way too long?!"

He finally put down his drink and looked back up at me. His eyes seemed regretful, yet determined. "I'm sorry, Misha. I don't know what else to say."

I stood there, also not knowing what I should say or do next. I was completely caught off-guard. And I hadn't expected this. I didn't know what he was talking about. I had thought that we had been happy. I had thought that everything between us had been great. I hadn't seen any warning signs...any red flags. And then it occurred to me...

"There's someone else?"

He shrugged. "There has been for a while."

I felt my legs giving out from under me as I leaned

back against the wall and then blindly reached for a chair. I sat down heavily and placed my face in my hands.

And then things went from bad to worse. "She's pregnant with my child."

I don't remember standing up. I don't remember reaching for the wine bottle. Nor do I remember tossing it against the wall so that shards of glass flew across the room and red wine began to spread across our pristine white carpet resembling a slow pool of blood. My blood, I thought to myself, since Wyatt had figuratively ripped my heart out.

Wyatt was now standing, his face showing surprise and fear. I had a temper, a really bad temper, but I kept it tightly controlled...most of the time.

"Get the fuck out of my house."

He looked stunned and held his hands out as if to defend himself from me. "Misha, I know you're angry. We should talk..." His words came out almost as a plea.

"There's nothing to talk about, you cheating piece of shit." My voice dripped with venom. I meant every word. Now when I looked at him I didn't see the handsome, tall, brilliant man I married. I saw a cheater, a no good shadow of a man. He sickened me.

"You're disgusting," I said simply. I didn't torture myself by asking how long his affair had been going on. I didn't want to know. And I also didn't care who he was having an affair with. All I knew is that he had been screwing around with someone else and now that someone else was pregnant.

"You made it clear that you never wanted kids---"

"How does that give you the right to go stick your dick in someone else?!" I screamed.

"Don't be so vulgar---"

"Vulgar? You're worried about me being vulgar? That's your concern, Wyatt? You know what concerns me?" He opened his mouth and then seemed to think better of it. Apparently, having an affair hadn't made him stupid. "My main concern is that you promised to share your life with me, but instead you cheated and started screwing around with someone else. So, I think I have a right to be vulgar. I have a right to be mad. So don't give me a lecture on vulgarity, you repulsive, spineless, sorry excuse for a man."

"It just happened...it wasn't planned."

"I don't care if your dick didn't have an itinerary. How does that make it any better? How is that an excuse to mess around on your wife? Your wife! I'm your wife, Wyatt! For eight years, I've been there for you. For eight years we've shared our lives! And now I find out that my husband, the person I thought I could trust with my life, has knocked up some other woman. How do you think that makes me feel, Wyatt? I'll tell you. Like shit."

I was done discussing anything with him as I

abruptly walked away. I headed toward our bedroom and walked straight to the window, opening it wide.

"What are you doing?" he asked, following me.

"You're just lucky I don't own a gun," I growled as I walked into his closet. I began ripping his clothes off the hangers and carried them in my arms and promptly threw them out of the window.

He reached out to stop me and I gave him a look that would stop death in its tracks. He promptly took a step back.

"Throwing out my belongings doesn't help any." He had the gall to sound offended.

"Being a cheating son of a bitch doesn't help any either," I said, gathering up another pile of clothes and happily watching them all float to the ground.

Mrs. Friedan, our nosey neighbor, of course, chose that moment to come by with her dog and looked up at the clothing floating through the air as I threw more out.

I waved happily and shouted from my window, "Hi, Mrs. Friedan. Don't mind the mess. My husband is sticking his penis in places that he shouldn't so I'm helping him move out."

"Misha!" Wyatt hissed, coming to stand next to me to look out of the window. Mrs. Friedan stared at us speechless while her dog did number two in our yard.

"I'm sorry, Mrs. Friedan. It's just a minor domestic

dispute, nothing to worry about," Wyatt assured her with a false smile. He shot me a glare, saying, "You're making a scene."

And I whispered threateningly to him, "Say one more word and you'll learn exactly what it feels like to fall out of a second storey window. You might be a hotshot engineer, but I'm pretty sure you haven't mastered the art of flight."

Mrs. Friedan was dragging her now urinating dog down the street. "Let's go, Twinkle. Come on, girl...let's go." She looked nervously up at us as if she were afraid to get sucked into our lunacy. And that's exactly what this situation was...lunacy.

Wyatt glared at me and stomped away from the window. "Great, Misha. Now the neighbors will think we're crazy."

"The neighbors? You care about the neighbors' opinion of you, but you're perfectly okay with me knowing that you're the lowest of the low? Check. Got it."

He frowned at me and shook his head as if he felt sorry for me. "I should have known better than to expect you to handle this maturely."

My fists tightened. Now I wish I had tossed him out of the window with his clothes.

"And I'm not leaving...you're the one who's leaving."

"What?" I was shocked. "This is my home and you have no right to make me leave."

"Do I have to call the authorities?"

"I dare you."

"You already have a record," he warned.

"For public nudity!" I had been a little bit wild in college to say the least.

"Still...let's not make this any harder than it has to be."

"What the---" I stopped abruptly as he reached for his cell phone and began dialing.

"Oh my god, are you seriously calling 911?"

He looked at me annoyed. "What do you think I am? Some sort of monster? I'm clearly calling the non-emergency number." God, I hated how he was still capable of being perfectly reasonable while I, on the other hand, was barely dealing with the fact that my world was falling apart.

I slapped the phone out of his hand and it went flying under our dresser.

I scrambled for it and while reaching for it I found a pair of bright pink panties. Panties that weren't my own.

I slowly stood up and extended the panties in front of me. "You brought her here?" My voice was now shaking and I realized my hands were shaking too.

"I'm not going to answer that," he said tightly and suddenly everything I felt for him, everything I thought

I felt for him began to change. He seemed smaller to me, less of a man. But my anger didn't dissipate. Oh no, I was just getting started.

"You're leaving now."

"I already told you--"

He stopped abruptly as I pulled my phone out of my pocket and began scrolling through my contacts list looking for a number.

"Who are you calling?"

"Uncle Niko," I said casually.

"Wwwwwwhat?" Wyatt stuttered. "Put down the phone. You're being ridiculous."

"Found it...dialing..." I said, putting the phone up to my ear.

"You're joking...right? You wouldn't. Fine! Fine! I'll leave!" he shouted, getting visibly upset. I hung up and said, "I thought you would."

Without a parting word, he turned on his heels and walked out of the bedroom. A minute later I heard the front door slam and I took a deep breath and lowered myself onto the bench that sat in front of our bed.

Our bed...I thought bitterly to myself. I wondered how many times he had defiled it. Now I wondered who the other woman was. All the fight in me was gone. I felt a tear slip down my cheek and wiped it away. I dared any other tears to fall. I wasn't a crier. I never had been and I wasn't planning to start now.

My marriage was over. My career was over. The life I had spent the past eight years building was gone. I stood up and realized I still had the panties in my hand. I tossed them out of the window and watched them hit the ground, falling on top of the rest of Wyatt's things.

And then I found another bottle of wine, sat on the couch and drank straight out of the bottle.

I took a few more sips and thought to myself, "Well, Misha, you've hit rock bottom...there's nothing but up from here."

And I prayed to whatever saint handled miracles, as I closed my eyes, that I would catch a break at least for the night. I was done for the day. A philandering husband. A baby by someone else. A business gone. Life was kicking my butt and today I was all out of fight. I picked up the wine bottle, grabbed my phone and made my way to the guest room determined to drown my troubles, at least for tonight, in a bottle of wine.

2

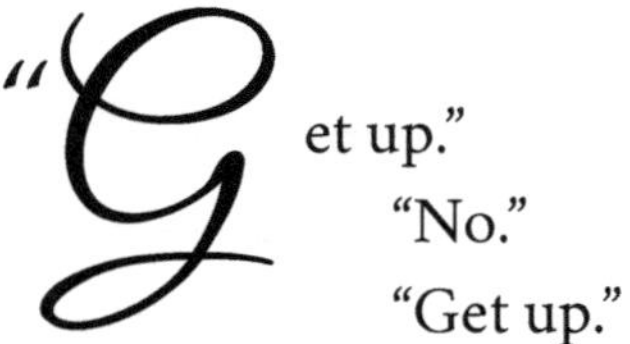

"Get up."

"No."

"Get up."

"Go away," I groaned as I tried to use my pillow to block out the burst of light that filled my room.

"You have two seconds to get up or I'm bringing in a hose."

I peeked out from under my pillow and said to the man who was standing next to my bed, looking annoyed, "Oh man...did Grandma call you?"

Uncle Niko nodded. "She says you haven't showered in weeks."

I sat up and shrugged. "It might have been that long. Maybe longer."

Uncle Niko shook his head and said, "Pitiful. You

look like a dirty, street kid. Like you spend your evenings picking through garbage looking for food."

I looked down at my shirt. I had fallen asleep in a t-shirt and sweatpants. It was my uniform now. My shirt was covered in mustard stains. I couldn't help myself. I binge ate hot dogs when I was depressed. And there were unknown stains all over my sweatpants. I figured some of those stains were ketchup, relish and probably even more mustard.

"Okay, so I eat like a pig when I'm depressed. Sue me. Whatever," I said, turning to bury myself back under the blankets when I caught sight of my face in the mirror. I had black smudges across my cheeks. "Where the heck did those come from?" I said to myself as I spit on my fingers and tried to wipe it off.

Uncle Niko sat down in the chair across from me and shook his head. He said with amusement, "You look like a coal miner."

He was right. "I have no idea what this gook is on my face." I gave up trying to fix it.

"You're a mess, Misha."

"My life is a mess. What do you expect?"

"I definitely don't expect you to just sleep your life away just because Wyatt left you. I never liked that guy."

I fell back on my bed with a sigh. "For the hundredth time...I left him. He did not leave me. Well, I mean...we left each other."

"Doesn't matter...same conclusion. You getting up sometime this week or do you plan to turn into a dry skeleton?" He shook his head. "I thought I raised you better."

"You didn't raise me."

"I gave you candy. And sent you birthday cards."

"Why'd you stop giving me candy?" I whined, feeling nostalgic for simpler times when my only concern had been how much chocolate I could stuff myself with.

"You're an adult. Buy your own candy."

"Newsflash, Uncle Niko. I'm broke."

He instantly stopped teasing me. "You serious?"

I turned my face to look at him. He hadn't aged much over the years, except that his dark hair was now turning slightly silver and there were silver streaks in his beard. He was short and stocky, wearing jeans and a plain t-shirt. He had tattoos from his wrists up both his arms, finishing at his neck. And he had a scar that started at the top of his forehead and finished just between his brows.

He wore his wedding ring on his finger. He never removed it, even though his wife, Selma, had been dead for at least two decades.

He looked tough because he was tough. I remember hearing rumors that he served time before I was born. And my friends in the neighborhood had said he was in the mafia. Grandma had always silenced those rumors, but just looking at him, it was an easy assumption to make. Most people who didn't know him well were afraid of him.

He was tough-looking on the outside and a tough talker too, but he had always been there for me and my friends. Embarrassingly enough, he had met all my dates. He had also scared all my dates away so it was a miracle that I had even ended up married.

"Maybe you should have done a better job scaring Wyatt away," I commented out loud.

"Huh?" he said, looking at me funny.

I sighed. "I was just thinking that you did such a great job during my teenage years scaring off all the boys, but somehow you let Wyatt slip through the cracks."

"He was always a pansy. I knew the moment I met him that he was bad news," Uncle Niko said. "You should have married that Kenny fella. He was a nice kid."

"He's gay," I said, knowing exactly who he was referring to. Kenny had been my high school crush. He also took me to prom...which is when I found out he was gay. I caught him making out with the quarterback and figured prom night wasn't working out in my favor. I guess I had a history of being involved with men who didn't want to be involved with me.

"No! Seriously?!" His eyes were round in surprise. "But he has a family!"

"Yeah, I heard he came out to his wife a few years ago and now he's married to his divorce lawyer. I heard they're very happy together; even Kenny's ex-wife is remarried. So, it all worked out. They all even still go to the same church."

"No kidding…" Uncle Niko said and then he looked at me with pity. "Did Wyatt leave you for another man too?"

"I'm pretty sure he left me for a woman, given that she's pregnant and all," I said, annoyed that Uncle Niko was bringing it up.

"You sure?"

I tossed a pillow at him and he easily dodged it, a big smile spreading across his face. "Still too slow---"

His smile disappeared as another one of my pillows caught him in the face.

"Now care to tell me what you're doing here?"

Here, I was embarrassed to say, was my grandmother's condo where I was hiding out from life. I wasn't taking any calls…I had even shut out my best friends, Lacey and Emmaline. They'd heard the whole sordid story from Grandma. Besides Grandma, Uncle Niko was the only person I'd spoken to since Wyatt sprung the news of his affair on me.

"Mom's concerned. She said you've been holed up in here for weeks. She's worried about you."

I frowned and slowly sat up. "She should have said something to me. Why did she call you?"

"Well, she figured you wouldn't speak to your parents and you refused to talk to Lacey and Emmaline..."

I shrugged it off. I didn't exactly get along with my parents. We never saw eye to eye on anything and that was why I had practically lived with my grandma in Brooklyn since I was a teen. I was named after my father actually. His name was Misha, a popular Russian male name which Mom thought would be a great fit for me. I wasn't bitter. I liked my name. It made me stand out. And I looked just like my dad.

He was petite for a man, not quite 5'5 with light blonde hair and green eyes. I was the same. I was only 5'1 and had the same pale complexion as my father. The same light hair. The same green eyes. The only thing I had inherited from my mom it seemed was her temper and demeanor. The difference was --- she was unapologetically mean. I at least tried to be nice.

My dad was a postman and my mom was a homemaker. She watched a lot of tv and shopped. Dad was pretty much a dictator and did what he wanted. He never spared anyone's feelings. They were perfect for each other and, in my opinion, they should never have had kids. I seemed to make them as miserable as they made me. It only took one fight, when my mom yelled out that she wished she had never had me, to make me realize that living with Granny was best for me. So, at 13, I had made the move and a few years after that, with a few court visits I had become an emancipated adult, legally free of my parents. Granny had been happy to have me. I think she had been lonely without me. I hadn't seen my parents in a few years, but I spoke to my mom every now and then when she called to check on Granny. She never checked on me. I figured she knew I would always be fine. She used to say that I had nine lives.

My Uncle Niko was my mom's brother. Growing up he had been like my replacement father; he filled in for my dad who expressed zero interest in me, unless it was to criticize me. Uncle Niko had been like my surrogate father figure for my formative years as well. I had him and Granny to thank for the fact that I had turned out so well. Well, at least, I kind of turned out well.

I mean, Wyatt's infidelity wasn't a reflection on me, right? I shook my head as if to shake the thought away. I wasn't going to be one of those women who blamed herself for her husband's infidelity.

"I'm okay. This is just my version of alone time. You shouldn't have come. I'm fine."

He looked over his shoulder and leaned toward me, whispering, "There's something else."

I sat up and said, "What? What's wrong?" I was concerned because Uncle Niko looked concerned. He never looked concerned.

"Wyatt called your grandmother today. I overheard them talking. Apparently, he's selling the condo."

"What?" I practically roared, jumping up from the bed. "That ass--"

"Hold it down. Hold it down," Uncle Niko said, looking over his shoulder again, but it was too late.

I could hear Grandma making her way to the guest bedroom. A few seconds later, she peeked in.

"What's with all the yelling?" she asked. Her blonde hair was completely white now and she wore glasses. She had a prominent nose and normally wore a serious expression. She didn't smile a lot, but she wasn't a bitter, humorless person. She just rarely smiled, so when she did smile it meant a lot. And besides that, she had a wicked sense of humor. She was my rock, always strong. Her expression never gave away what she was thinking. I was quick to anger and quick to speak, but she was always thoughtful and in control of her emotions. I envied her that.

"Why didn't you tell me?" were the first words out of my mouth before I could even think.

She shot Uncle Niko a meaningful look and he shrugged. "I can't keep a secret. I know, I know."

"It's not something you should worry about," she said, looking back at me.

"Not something I should worry about? He's selling your home!" I said a few choice words and my grandmother waited until I was done. For some reason, she didn't mind me cursing around her, even though I'd never heard her use such language before.

"We'll figure something out. I'll get a job. Rent an apartment."

"You're old! That's not going to happen!" I said, sounding panicked. Then I immediately felt bad. "Sorry," I mumbled.

"Don't be sorry. I am old, but there has to be something I can do."

"Grandma, I admire your "can-do" spirit, but I'm 30 and unable to find a job because people think I'm old. I think at 80, it might prove a bit more challenging."

"Nonsense," she said, "I can still drive. I can be an Uber driver or something."

Uncle Niko and I looked at each other. Living in New York City all her life, Grandma didn't get a license until she was around 60. And honestly, being in the car with her was still kind of scary.

"Let's wait on the whole job thing. I can't believe this.

How long do we have until her lousy ex sells this place?" Uncle Niko asked.

"He already sold it. He gave me until the end of the month to find someplace else," Grandma answered.

My mouth was agape. "The end of the month!" I sputtered. "That's in less than two weeks!"

The injustice and stress of the situation made my stomach turn. "I'm sorry, Grandma. This is all my fault."

When I had relocated to Florida after college, my grandmother had already been here. She had grown tired of the New York winters and had moved to Florida shortly after I graduated from college. She had ended up renting a small condo in a very diverse, up-and-coming neighborhood. As a surprise, Wyatt had bought the condo from its owner and gifted it to my grandmother. I had thought he had done it because he adored her too, but he had explained to me how it was one of many properties he had invested in for a very healthy return. That was Wyatt…always practical.

So, for almost 6 years, I had been paying the basic bills my grandmother had like utilities and cable. I hadn't thought about what would happen after I lost the business since I was so busy getting over the fact that he had betrayed me.

And apparently, he was betraying me again. More than betraying me. He was throwing an old woman out of her home.

"I'm going to talk to him. I'll convince him to reconsider," I said, feeling beyond guilty.

My grandmother shook her head and said with a steely voice, "No. We don't need his charity. I never wanted to accept it anyway."

She was right. She had at first refused to accept Wyatt's gift, but I had insisted she take it. After all, Wyatt was *family*. But now Wyatt wasn't family. Wyatt was a creep and now the magnitude of what he'd done made its way to my brain. The guilt from knowing my grandmother could be homeless all because of me was crushing.

I was normally too proud to beg, but my grandmother was reason enough for me to be willing to swallow my pride. I was seriously considering calling Wyatt and begging him to let Granny keep the condo.

Uncle Niko and Grandma left to go talk some more. I just sat there wondering what I should do next. I decided then to go for a drive, to clear my head. I didn't even get out of the parking lot. I was so overwhelmed that I couldn't even think straight. I felt like I was drowning and needed help. I couldn't do this alone anymore. I needed my friends.

I pulled out my cell phone and called Lacey.

"Hey, you," I said when she picked up.

"Oh my gosh, I'm so happy you called. I was just thinking about you! How are you?"

I sighed. "As good as can be expected."

"I never really liked Wyatt," Lacey said hotly. "Oliver feels the same way."

I smiled to myself. Oliver was Lacey's father-in-law. He doted on her like she was his own biological daughter. He was eccentric, an avid speed walker, and the most generous person I knew. He had formerly been her employer, but she had married his son under rather unconventional circumstances in Vegas. Safe to say, what happened in Vegas didn't stay in Vegas.

"Oliver barely knew Wyatt," I laughed.

"True, but he hated him instantly."

"Tell her I hate him with the fire of a thousand suns!" I heard Oliver yell in the background.

"Um...tell him thank you, I guess?" I felt myself coming out of a fog for the first time in weeks. "Oliver's great."

And just like that, I was ready to talk. I started to unload on Lacey about Grandma and how she was going to lose her home.

After I finished, Lacey simply said, "I knew Wyatt wouldn't exactly win a humanitarian of the year award since he abhors poor people and the elderly, but this is beyond spiteful even for him. This is such a heavy conversation. I think we should get Emmaline in on this. How about we all meet for dinner?"

I agreed and then lowered the sun visor to look at

myself in the mirror. Yep, still hideous, I thought to myself, pushing it back up. I sighed and headed back into the condo to take a shower, brush my teeth, and at least try to be presentable.

A few hours later I found myself pulling up to the entrance of Oliver's mansion. I parked my car and got out. Oliver didn't permit cars on the property. Like I mentioned, he was an eccentric man. I saw Emmaline's car as well. Great, all my pals are here, I thought to myself, already feeling better than I had in weeks.

I waved to Mr. Nguyen, his long-time guard, and he happily waved back as he opened the gate. I hiked up to the house, which sat about a quarter of a mile away from the road. As I headed up, I heard a noise. A motorcycle was heading in my direction. It zoomed by me, startling me, and I leaped back. So, motorcycles were okay, but not cars? Oliver was so random. As I set eyes on the mansion, I still felt the same awe as I did when I first saw it. It was a stunning work of art, an awe-inspiring estate. The architect had clearly put his heart and soul into it. But even though the mansion was intimidating on the outside and fit for a royal family, it felt like home because Oliver had always been so welcoming. In fact, when Lacey had mentioned dinner, Oliver had insisted that we meet up at his home and Lacey and I hadn't felt any need to argue with him.

When I finally arrived at the house I saw the motorcycle parked in front of it. Oliver stood in front of the grand entrance talking to the guy who I had seen earlier. He still held his helmet in his hand.

"There she is!" Oliver said upon seeing me.

I looked behind me and realized that he was talking about me. Why was he so excited to see me? He must have something up his sleeve, I thought, narrowing my eyes. Oliver was always full of surprises and I had no interest in being on the receiving end of one of them.

"Hi, Oliver." He happily made his way to my side. He was wearing very brief, tight-fitting shorts and a mesh, muscle-tee. I had to bite my lip to not giggle. Oliver's muscle mass was pretty nonexistent, so the muscle-tee was very baggy on him.

He offered me an arm and I looked up at the man who was waiting at the top of the steps for us. Whoever Oliver's friend was...he was totally hot. With that thought in mind, I immediately missed a step and fell forward directly on top of Oliver.

I was mortified as the handsome stranger gracefully made his way down to us. Oliver and I were a tangle of arms and legs as we attempted to extract our limbs from under each other. The motorcycle guy extended a hand and tried to pull me up. I was afraid that all those hot dogs had added to my bulk. Not that I was fat, but I definitely could stand to lose about ten pounds...probably

15 now. After all, I had been spending the past few weeks just stuffing my face.

"Erik," Oliver said, gasping for air as I attempted to crawl off of him. "This is the girl I wanted you to meet. This is Misha."

The guy called Erik gave me a stiff polite smile and, with a little pull, completely pulled me off of Oliver's body. It wasn't until I was fully pulled up that I realized I had had my knee in Oliver's belly. Poor guy.

"Thanks, Erik. I'm usually pretty graceful," I lied.

"I'm sure you are." His dark eyes were unsmiling and he seemed like he wanted to be anywhere else but there. It was impossible not to notice how attractive he was. In fact, he was probably the most attractive man I had ever seen in my life. He had dark brown eyes, full lips, and could easily have been a Hollywood actor stepping off a movie set. He looked French to me with his cool look. He wore a light tan colored shirt that fit tightly across his upper body. He was built like a swimmer, tall with long lean muscles in his arms but with a broad, heavily muscular chest. He was clearly in shape, I thought as I looked at his impossibly flat stomach, narrow waist and long legs, almost too muscular for his slim fitting pants.

"Misha, I was just telling Erik about your issue. And you guys might be the key to each other's problems."

"Excuse me?" I said, clearly not understanding.

"Your money problem."

I blushed. Oliver was the worst! He knew nothing about what topics were socially inappropriate. Actually, he did know, he just didn't care. "Did Lacey tell you everything?" Gosh, I hoped not.

"Of course, she did. Once she gets upset about something the whole household doesn't hear the last of it."

I groaned. And then I looked at Erik. "So, what's your story?"

"My story is that I'm leaving now."

I was taken aback by his abruptness. "Well, by all means, don't let little old me stand in your way."

He immediately looked contrite. "I apologize for my rudeness. I'd just rather not discuss my personal affairs with a stranger."

"What personal affairs?" I asked, now more curious than I was before. What was Erik so against discussing with a stranger? And why had Oliver wanted me to meet him?

"Misha isn't a stranger. She's practically family," Oliver said as he attempted to right himself. I offered a hand down and he took it.

"Nevertheless, Oliver, I would appreciate your discretion regarding the matter."

Oliver shook his head. "I think you're making a mistake. You should let me help you. I'm good at this!"

Good at what? I thought, even more intrigued.

Erik shrugged. "You have a right to your opinion,

even if I don't agree with it." His tone was matter-of-fact.

"It was nice meeting you, Misha." And with that he walked off. He got on the back of his motorcycle and drove off.

I immediately turned to Oliver, "What was that about?"

Oliver chewed his bottom lip as if trying to decide how much to not tell me. "I'll get him to tell you later. Go on inside. I'll join you soon," he said ushering me in. "Lacey is probably worried you got lost in the bushes or something."

His garden was like a labyrinth so getting lost in it wasn't quite an exaggeration, but as I made my way to the door, I couldn't help but wonder about the sexy guy now driving away on his motorcycle, as if the devil himself was after him.

3

I didn't feel like celebrating. I felt like hiding under my pillows, but I had done that too much over the past few weeks. My savings were drying up and I just felt so lost. Grandma was staying with a friend and her stuff was all in storage until we figured out what to do next. Uncle Niko had headed back up to New York. I was all alone in my misery. I had considered bunking on Emmaline's couch, but decided against it. Instead I was alternating between sleeping in the monstrosity that used to be Wyatt's and my home and living in Oliver's pool house, depending on the given night. Being in the house reminded me of my failed marriage and, per the divorce agreement, Wyatt got the house anyway. I was just buying time until he sold it from right under me like he had done with Grandma's condo. I felt ridiculous, not knowing what to do next and at the mercy of my ex.

I felt as if my security blanket had been ripped right from underneath me and the world was again the hostile place I remembered it to be when I was 13. When I wasn't hiding from my problems, I was on the internet. I had started applying to jobs and only received rejection letters thus far from the few interior design shops that were hiring. I could feel the weight of the world on my shoulders as I raised my hand to knock on the front door of Lacey and Jude's loft. The doorbell had been broken for a while, but they were too cheap to get it fixed. They were billionaires, but too cheap to fix their doorbell. I guess that's how billionaires stay billionaires, by spending as little as possible.

I heard someone opening the door and was surprised to see Emmaline standing there. She had beat me to the party. "Hi, stranger!" she said before embracing me tightly and I sighed against her shoulder and lightly hugged her back.

She pulled away and asked me, "Are you feeling okay? I'm sorry I haven't had the chance to stop by to see you."

"Don't apologize. You have a life. A daughter. A husband. One friend going through a life crisis doesn't need all your attention."

"But still, I feel terrible. Are you doing any better?"

I lied. "Yes, a little." I didn't want her worrying about me. I was used to taking care of my friends and helping them get out of sticky situations, but for some reason I couldn't ask them to do the same for me. It made me feel weak.

I knew I shouldn't feel that way. They would do anything for me. Emmaline and Lacey had been my best friends since college. They had been two country girls and I had found them warm and authentic, a welcome difference from the girls we went to college with who had never left Manhattan. Emmaline had even gotten pregnant during college and had been ready to quit indefinitely, but I had arranged for her to stay with my grandmother who had become like a stand-in grandma for both my friends.

"What's Granny going to do now? I heard about that jerk Wyatt selling her home."

I shook my head. "I don't know. She's staying with a friend in a senior community. It seems like she's having a blast actually. They're always out antiquing or exercising."

"Well, you and Grandma are always welcome at my house."

I knew she meant it, but I didn't want to inconvenience her too. Oliver was already too kind for letting me stay in his pool house. It had been months since the day I found out Wyatt was cheating on me, but our divorce had only been finalized for a week at most.

The loft was one big open space. I passed by the table where we were about to have dinner and made my way to the kitchen to see if Lacey needed help.

As I looked around, I was surprised at how clean the loft was. Lacey complained on a daily basis that Jude was a bit of a slob. I guess she had made him clean up before the big party. There were even tiki lamps around which made me giggle. But there were no signs of dirty dishes, old socks, or pizza boxes, which Lacey said frequently appeared whenever she left Jude at home alone.

"Hey, Lacey," I said as I spotted her in the kitchen.

"Hi! So glad you're here," she said, coming over to embrace me. They were the only people I readily hugged besides my grandmother. I didn't come from an affectionate family.

"Can I help?"

She looked around and it really seemed like she had everything under control. I think she came to that same conclusion.

"Go ahead and sit down or mingle. I have everything ready."

"You can take this, though." She handed me green beans. I sat them on the table when the front door opened again. Knowing it was just Oliver, I ignored it and focused on helping with setting the plates up for dinner.

As I placed another plate on the table, I looked up and saw Emmaline open the door to Oliver and behind Oliver was Erik. I was surprised. I glanced down at his hand and noticed Erik wasn't carrying his helmet today. That was too bad, I thought, it made him look extra sexy.

He made his way around the room talking with Emmaline and Colin. He even joked around with Lacey while I finished up some last-minute place settings.

I watched him watch me as he came around the table to the only available seat. And of course, we ended up sitting right next to each other.

Oliver started talking enthusiastically as he sat down across from me. "Misha, so glad that you're here. I looked for you at the pool house to see if you wanted to ride with Erik and me. Anyway, so like I was saying the other day, Erik here needs a ----"

"Personal assistant," Erik said quickly, cutting off Oliver who looked at him funny.

I wondered what that look was all about.

"I need a personal assistant. Oliver here is going out of his way to make sure I find one."

"Misha could do it," Lacey volunteered happily. I looked from Lacey back to my plate, back to Lacey.

"I'm sorry, what are we talking about?"

"Erik needs a personal assistant. You need a job, so it might just work out."

"I'm not qualified to be a personal assistant," I said slightly offended. "I'm an interior designer."

"Didn't Erik just buy a home? You should totally hire Misha. She'll make it look amazing," Lacey kept going and I was beginning to feel embarrassed. Finally, it was becoming clear that I was a matchmaking target. It was like everyone was conspiring to get us together, but I truly didn't understand why. I was a boring divorcee, not a trophy wife. And isn't that what Erik and his type liked?

"I'm sure Erik has someone already."

"Actually, I don't, but I am interested. Maybe you can take a look and give me some ideas."

I was taken aback. Wow, just like that? Who needed Internet job boards when you could just network for an opportunity? Maybe matchmaking wasn't so bad.

"Maybe you can make it feel like a home. It's just a blank slate now. It's gorgeous though. Perfect for me. And most of it has already been renovated." His eyes lit up as he began to talk about his home. Apparently, he had already put a lot of energy and money into making it his own. But of course, I was assuming he did the work himself and didn't hire out. If Erik was a friend of Oliver's then he was probably richer than anyone I'd ever met. Maybe he was even wealthier than Oliver. I paused thinking, was that even possible? Oliver was pretty loaded.

"I, uhhh...that sounds great." I couldn't believe my luck, but then I remembered that the dinner wasn't about me. "I'd love to hear more. Want to talk about it after dinner?"

"Sure," he said. Not only was he gorgeous, but he was also not a jerk. And I was attracted to him. Uh oh.

Finally, Jude, Lacey's husband showed up. After a wild night in Vegas, they had married and to everyone's surprise stayed married.

I sort of envied their relationship. I had never looked at Wyatt the way Lacey looked at Jude. If I were to be honest, my relationship with Wyatt had always been less than passionate. I understood that a great love affair didn't define all marriages, but mine definitely never had a spark.

I had married Wyatt immediately after college. I had met him at a conference while we were both finishing up our sophomore years. It had been a conference for science majors. I had thought I was going to be a chemistry major until I realized it meant studying and there was no way I was going to waste my college years with my nose in a book. But Wyatt had been really into his engineering ideas and had won a prestigious scholarship. He had even submitted his business plan to several competitions and won them all, which gave him seed money to start his own business as soon as we gradu-ated. I had focused on teaching right after college. I regrettably hadn't majored in anything worthwhile and had instead earned a degree in liberal arts, which quali-fied me to do absolutely nothing. I had found that out the hard way after college when I couldn't find a job. It was like my jobless history was repeating itself, except television had propelled me into interior design the first time around.

Sitting at home one evening while Wyatt was working late, I had found myself watching a home design show and I knew instantly that's what I wanted to do. I had called the local community college the next day and signed up for classes. The rest, as they say, was history.

I had started off by taking a few clients here and there, mostly staging jobs, and then as my reputation grew so did my clients. I was earning enough to start my own firm. It had been a great five years and then slowly my business started to fade. I saw Erik's offer as a life-line. If I were able to get his business, surely others of his ilk would hire me to do their homes. I was finally seeing a light at the end of the tunnel.

"So why are we here again?" Erik surprised me by asking.

I raised a brow. "Aren't you a friend of the family's?"

"Yeah, but I just got back into the country and I can

barely keep up with checking my email, let alone remember all the causes and charities my friends support."

"You must have a ton of friends."

"Not really, I'm kind of a loner.

"Really? You seem like an extrovert."

He shook his head. "I don't have much confidence in theories about personality types, but I guess if I had to describe myself, I would say that I'm a well-socialized introvert."

I smiled. "Well-socialized introvert? Hmm...interesting. Anyway, we're here to celebrate Ophelia's Angels going international. Still want to stick around?" I teased.

He nodded. "Definitely. I can't believe Ophelia's Angels is going international. That's a cause that's dear to all of us. I'm glad you took the time to be here for Jude and Oliver." He smiled at me then and gone was the serious demeanor that I had encountered on the front porch of the mansion. His smile seemed to transform him. It made him more attractive, if that was even possible, and it made him seem younger. If I hazarded a guess, I would think he was between mid to late 30s.

I admonished myself for finding him attractive. Cool it, Misha. You're just a few months out of a failed marriage. And honestly, the last thing I needed to do was get involved with someone. I was still living with friends, didn't have a real home to call my own, and was technically unemployed. I felt like a charity case suddenly.

Jude greeted everyone at the table and then sat down quickly.

Oliver stood up, picked up a wine glass and everyone else followed. "I'd like to dedicate this toast to my son," Oliver said with a twinkle in his eye. "I thought he was a womanizing miscreant---"

"Thanks for that, Dad," Jude said sarcastically.

Oliver shot him a glare. "Let me finish, son. You're so quick to talk, you might try listening for once."

I wanted to roll my eyes, but I stopped myself because I didn't want to be rude. Jude and Oliver were always at each other's throats. It was almost as if arguing was how they expressed their love.

"Like I was saying before I was so rudely interrupted," he pointedly narrowed his eyes at Jude who held back a chuckle, "my son surprised me. He made this old man realize that people aren't always who they seem or who they pretend to be. He showed me that everyone has depth. He taught me that we're complicated beings, us humans, and we should never judge or assume we know the reality of others. Was he a womanizer and a miscreant?"

"Yep," said Lacey, answering the rhetorical question. This time Jude outright laughed.

"Okay, well yes, he was all those things, but I realized

he's also hardworking, compassionate, entrepreneurial, and a saint for putting up with me all these years without reinforcements," Oliver finished.

"Amen to that," Jude said, making the rest of us chuckle.

"Well, I know I'm not easy. And I want to thank Jude anyway for putting up with me. And I want to thank him for keeping his mother's memory alive. Your mother was a wonderful person and you're following in her footsteps with all the great work you did establishing and growing Ophelia's Angels in her honor. She would be proud of you, of all the good you're doing. I'm proud of you. I don't deserve a son like you. Thanks for putting up with this old fool."

Everyone was shocked by Oliver's sincere words. He was always a blunt person, but he didn't really talk about his feelings or show much emotion.

I looked up at Jude, as I swallowed back the lump that had formed in my throat, knowing that my parents would never say the same to me, and watched as Jude wordlessly stood up, crossed around the table and gave his dad a hug. He kissed him on the top of his bald head and then said, "Sit down, old man. We're not here to listen to your excuses for years of inadequacies. That's for your therapist. Let's eat."

We all chuckled, including Oliver, and began to pass

around the food when Lacey started hitting her glass with her fork.

She smiled widely as if she had a secret to tell and she just couldn't wait to tell us. "I also have something to say."

"Oh god, not you too. Not another heartfelt speech. What happened to my stoic, emotionless family? Who are these aliens that have replaced them?" lamented Jude.

"Hush you," Lacey said softly. "While we're all here, I wanted to make an announcement." She took a deep breath, looked around at all of us and shook her glass at us. "There's apple cider in here, not champagne...Who wants to guess why?"

I frowned, not understanding. "Oh, for goodness sake, don't tell me you gave up drinking. Now who am I going to go to happy hour with?" I was suddenly feeling cross.

Lacey smiled furtively. "We can go to happy hour together in about six months...if I can find a nanny!" She said the nanny part in a sing-song voice.

My eyes widened at the same time as Emmaline's. "Oh my god! You're pregnant," we said simultaneously.

We both then jumped up and hugged her. The guys got up and congratulated Jude.

Oliver kept blubbering, "I'm going to be a grandfather. A grandfather. Finally! Miracles do happen!"

Excited chatter about Lacey's announcement filled the room. Lacey and Jude kept smiling at each other. It was pretty adorable. And before I knew it, we were all done with our food. I said my goodbyes occupied by the news Lacey just dropped on us.

Yes, I was happy for her, but I didn't really share in her excitement. I wasn't ever the type of woman who dreamt about her domestic future. I never really dreamt about what my wedding would be like or what my apartment after college would look like. I just pretty much lived in the moment and let life take me wherever. Lacey was the opposite. If she could plan her own funeral posthumously, she would.

As a woman who never wanted kids, or ever fantasized about a family, it was hard for me to relate to the whole excitement over becoming a mom. After all, it's not like being a mom had ever made my mom happy. The only photo I'd ever seen of her smiling was taken years before I was born. And every photo afterward featured her looking tired and unhappy. Despite this, I never felt my mom didn't love me, I just felt that she didn't have the energy or emotional aptitude to show it.

When I had dated Wyatt, we hadn't discussed children. It had come as a surprise years later when he'd suggested that we try for a baby, that someone like him would even want kids. He was so uptight, so controlling that I didn't think someone with his personality would ever contemplate having children. There would just be too many unknowns that a parent couldn't control. He had been shocked to know that I hadn't wanted to have any. And I had felt guilty for years for depriving him of a child of his own. But he had assured me that wanting children had just been on his "To-do" list so to speak. A role that he had assumed he would perform, and so he hadn't pushed the issue. He had been disappointed, yes, but he told me he would get over it, that he was too practical to get emotionally distraught over something that we hadn't even agreed on.

And now he was about to be a father. I briefly thought to myself that maybe if I had given him a baby, more of a family life, he would have come home to me instead of his mystery woman. If I hadn't been tied up with building my business, then losing my business, and if instead I had focused on home and babies, we would still be together. But I knew it was silly to torture myself with what-ifs.

A baby wouldn't have saved our relationship. I knew that. A baby would have just meant another innocent person being hurt by our failed marriage.

I was so deep in thought as I made my way to my car that I didn't hear the footsteps behind me until the person touched my shoulder.

I turned around ready to fight and scream when I saw that it was Erik standing there.

"Woah, don't punch me. I didn't mean to startle you. I tried calling out to you, but you didn't answer."

I placed my hand over my heart. "You scared me half way to death, you loser."

He laughed. "I'm sorry...did you just call me a loser?"

I placed my hands on my hips. "Yes. That's exactly what I called you."

"You're feisty."

"So I've been told. So, what can I do for you? Why are you running around stalking me in the middle of the night?"

He laughed. "We were supposed to discuss working together, remember? But if you would rather not take my money..." He let his voice trail off.

I drew my brows close together, in deep thought, and then I remembered! "Oh my god! I'm an idiot. Hell yeah, I want your money."

He laughed, I guess not expecting that response.

I had been so focused on Lacey's news that I'd forgotten I was supposed to talk to Erik after dinner. What a disaster. I was a disaster.

"I mean I would love to discuss with you what your plans are for your house. I'm sure we can come up with something pretty great between the two of us."

The second those words left my mouth I wanted to just jump in my car and leave. I couldn't believe I had just said that. "Come up with something pretty great between the two of us?" What the hell? Was I coming on to him? I mean, I loved sex and was going through a sexual drought, but surely I wasn't so needy that I was subconsciously interjecting innuendos in my speech.

"I think that's a great idea," he said without any hesitation. I guess he didn't think I was propositioning him. Good. Because I wasn't. Maybe. My subconscious really couldn't be trusted.

"How about I give you a call tomorrow when we're both more awake? I'm kind of exhausted and I'm afraid my thoughts aren't coming out very clearly."

"I understand the feeling. Tonight was kind of a lot. I mean, Lacey's announcement sent me whirling," he said unexpectedly. "She's going to be a mom. I understand her excitement."

"Really? Are you a parent yourself?"

He shook his head. "No. But maybe one day..." His voice held a wistfulness as he said that.

I didn't know how to respond to his comment, so I smoothly changed the subject to a topic I was more comfortable discussing: business. "Here, let me give you my number."

"No need. Oliver already did," he said. His face was illuminated by the full moon and I tried not to stare at his lips. I think I failed as I watched his full lips pull back into a knowing smile. I forced myself to meet his eyes as he said, "I'll call you soon, Misha. And Oliver was right, I would have regretted not seeing you tonight."

With those cryptic words, he wished me goodnight and strolled to his car. It was a low sports car. The type of car I had always wanted to drive. And he owned one. Lucky bastard.

"Oliver, you sneaky matchmaker, what have you done?" I said to myself, as I made my way to my practical sedan. I secretly believed that Oliver had been trying to pair Lacey with Jude from the very start and now I felt he might also be meddling in my love affairs. I sighed. What was I going to do about that sneaky, little old man?

4

I didn't wear a bra. I'm not sure what I was thinking, but I didn't wear one. I looked down at myself and sighed. So much for NOT being a disaster.

It was hot and I had grabbed the first thing out of my closet. I was dressed like I was going to go hang out at the beach.

I had on a large straw sun hat, dark red lipstick that looked great on my pale complexion and I was wearing an off-white skater dress with spaghetti straps. I looked great, as if I were going on a casual date. But I was actually trying to land a client. I was seriously off my game. I was starting to wonder if Wyatt's betrayal had done more than just hurt me emotionally. I just felt like I had nothing but bad luck after bad luck, as if I were engaging in some form of self-sabotage on a subconscious level.

Erik stood up as I approached him. He smiled at me and extended his hand. Not thinking, I took it and he pulled me into his arms, hugging me briefly before letting me go. He still held on to my hand though as he studied me, with clear approval in his eyes. "If you wore that outfit to get my attention, then you definitely have it."

I snatched my hand away and said, "I'm not interested in attracting you, Erik." I instantly regretted my sharp tone; clearly, he was only joking. I opened my mouth to apologize, but he was still talking...

"That's too bad because it's working," he said, making me feel flattered despite my annoyance.

I decided to tell him so. "That's really nice of you to say, but let's cut to the chase. This will be strictly business."

"I don't know, business and pleasure kind of go hand in hand, don't you think? I know I get a certain pleasure from making money."

I shrugged. "I never thought of it that way." I never had much disposable income before. My fun money mostly went to saving and making sure I provided my grandma with everything she needed. I was grateful that I had saved though, otherwise I would be depending on my friends for a lot more than just a roof over my head while I figured out what to do with my life.

That reminded me. I knew nothing about Erik. It was important for me to learn about my clients, to understand their likes and dislikes. What I knew about Erik was pretty basic. I just knew that he was flirtatious, friendly, and apparently keeping a secret that only Oliver seemed to know. For some reason, that made him even more appealing to me. A girl liked a little mystery.

"So, Erik, what's your story?"

"My story?"

"Yep. What do you do for starters and where are you from?"

"How is that relevant to your work? Shouldn't you just be asking me what my favorite color is and whether or not I prefer traditional or modern design?"

He signaled for a waitress and took it upon himself to order a couple of drinks for the two of us. He was a gentleman though and double checked that what he ordered worked for me. I liked a man that took charge but also cared enough for my opinion. If Oliver was trying to set us up, then he had definitely found a winner in my eyes. So far Erik was impressive, from his looks to his personality. He intrigued me and maybe someone like Erik was exactly what I needed after being treated like dirt by Wyatt.

"Come on, Erik. Humor me. I need to get in your

head, understand your likes and dislikes. I need to know what makes you tick in order to design rooms that you'll love. So yeah, I need to know more than just your favorite color is green and you hate mid-century furniture."

"How'd you know that?" he said teasingly, but his expression remained dubious. "Just make the house inviting and cozy. There's no need to understand me at all. I barely understand me most days."

"You love to contradict people and make things harder than they need to be, don't you?"

"That's my specialty."

"Well, you're not getting away with it today."

"Come on, my favorite color is green, you know." The waiter returned and gave us our drinks. He tipped his glass toward me and said, "Cheers to a wonderful working relationship with a truly intriguing woman."

I added to the toast saying, "Cheers to a wonderful working relationship with a truly elusive and somewhat annoying man."

He chuckled and put his glass down without taking a sip. He leaned his elbows on the table, his face coming just inches from mine, and said, "It seems like I've met my match." He gave me a devilish grin that instantly made me grin too. I felt my nipples harden and his eyes looked down my blouse. I knew he couldn't see my breasts, but a lot of me was on display.

He slowly sat back and studied me, never breaking eye contact as he took a sip from his glass. "I like this. Let's see how this partnership goes. Let's shake on it."

He extended his hand and I ignored it. "No. Let's not shake on it. Let's sign on it."

"My handshake isn't good enough?"

"No, I would definitely prefer money…wire transfer…stocks and bonds maybe?"

He laughed. "You're hilarious."

"I try. So what's your story? How many times do I need to ask before you tell?"

"Alright, alright," he said. He took a sip of his drink again and then started to talk. "Let's start with the basics. I'm in real estate. I started off as a contractor, flipping houses. I ended up flipping million-dollar homes. Made some smart investments. And now I'm here." He gestured toward the restaurant. "Here in the presence of a beautiful lady."

"You're a shameless flirt. And I feel like none of it is sincere." Although I secretly hoped at least part of it was. It was nice to have the attention of a man. Whether I admitted it or not, Wyatt's betrayal had even impacted my self-esteem. I found myself now questioning my looks, my decisions, my feelings about people. I was second guessing myself at every turn.

"Sincerity isn't my strongest quality."

"Or even a quality you possess?" I teased.

"Ha ha."

"You and Jude have a similar sense of humor. How do you know Oliver and Jude?"

"I tried to rob Oliver once."

I blinked and smiled uncertainly...assuming he was joking, but I didn't get the punch line.

"What? Explain."

He settled back in his chair, as if getting comfortable.

Uh oh. This is going to be a doozy, I said to myself.

He opened his mouth, ready to speak, thought better of it and then shook his head. "That's a story for another day. Suffice it to say, Jude, Oliver and I are now good friends, but we met under less than ideal circumstances."

"Less than ideal circumstances, huh? Care to elaborate?"

"Care to stop being nosey?"

"Being nosey is my job."

"I feel like you're a journalist and I need to tell you to keep all this off the record. You aren't secretly a journalist just trying to get a story on Florida's most eligible bachelor?"

"You think very highly of yourself...for all we know you could be Florida's least eligible bachelor."

"You're lucky I have a healthy dose of self-esteem or that comment would have me in the bathroom crying right now."

"There's still time for that."

He laughed, clearly not having expected that comment.

"Okay, you've bested me verbally so far. Anyway," he said, leaning back appraising me with a smile on his face, "is being intrusive a prerequisite for being an interior decorator?"

"Well, if you think about it, I do invite myself into other people's homes and pretty much violate their privacy while I make things beautiful."

"You have a point. Your parents must be very proud."

Ugh...my parents...not a subject I wanted to talk about. I decided not to comment on them and continued my train of thought.

I said, "So tell me about your home. What would you like done to it? What's your style?"

He pulled out his phone and said, "I can do better than that. I can show you my home. And I can show you pictures of things I like, rooms that I think would be cool in my home." He brought his chair around until he was sitting directly next to me. I don't know why, but his nearness made my skin flush. I was much too aware of him for decency's sake.

I had a very bad habit of sweating when I was socially uncomfortable, and I begged my underarms not to betray me by sweating profusely. I thanked god that I had actually had the insight to shave them. Truth be told, now that Wyatt and I weren't a couple, I had let certain "maintenance" duties fall by the wayside. Until this morning, I hadn't shaved my legs in weeks and other things…I hadn't shaved at all.

Not that Erik would find that out. It wasn't as if he were going to put his hand up my dress or anything. Not that I would mind if he did...

I realized then that Erik was talking and I had been too busy thinking about the feel of his hand going up my dress to pay attention to the conversation that I was presently included in.

"I'm sorry. I had something on my mind and that took my attention," I gave him a small smile, hoping that he wouldn't ask what exactly had been on my mind. Now that would make for an awkward conversation.

And of course I was unlucky. "What exactly were you thinking about? You look a little...flushed?" His eyes were teasing and I wanted to hit him for guessing so easily. For all my quick wit and flirtatious ways, I was an innocent. Wyatt had been the only man I had seriously dated and then we had married quickly. All the men I flirted with in the design business were pretty safe given that most of them had been gay.

Erik was definitely not safe. Far from it. Erik could get me into trouble, but as I thought of what to say, I couldn't help but think that maybe trouble was exactly what I needed.

"It's none of your business what I'm thinking about," I finally said.

"Oh really? Then it must have been especially dirty."

I looked at him and immediately began to laugh. "You're the dirty one, Erik," I said once I was able to catch my breath.

He shrugged. "If only you knew."

I prayed my nipples weren't betraying me again and was grateful that he was sitting next to me instead of across from me. I knew they were probably poking at the thin fabric of my dress. They were such attention hogs. God, if I hadn't been married, I would have been such a slut, I thought with an internal laugh. There's still time for that...I thought to myself before focusing again on the task at hand.

I then leaned toward him and we began to scroll through the pictures of his home together. It wasn't a grand mansion like Oliver's place. In fact, it wasn't much bigger than the home Wyatt and I had shared, but I was going to transform Erik's house into more than just a showpiece, it was going to be a real home after I was done with it. A sanctuary, a place where you went for comfort at the end of your day. It was going to be great. When I was done, he would never want to leave it.

"Where is it? Where's your home located?" From what I could gather from the pictures, it seemed to be off somewhere, situated away from the rest of the world.

"An island. I bought it from a retired captain. It's off of Key West, on its own island practically, surrounded by wildlife. It's on an oasis. A little bit of paradise."

And he was right. It was definitely a little bit of paradise. This was probably going to be my biggest, but most fun challenge. I didn't have a whole design team, so I would need to do all the planning and grunt work myself. That meant making all the arrangements for the laborers, ordering supplies, doing all the shopping...I felt overwhelmed, but excited at the same time.

I began to tell Erik all the ideas I had for his place and he nodded enthusiastically, adding when I was done, "You should accompany me for the weekend, you know, get a feel for the place."

"Accompany you for the weekend? You mean spend the night?"

Erik comically raised his brows and said mockingly, "Misha, you move so fast. I would love for you to spend the night, but you should at least take me to dinner first."

I shook my head. "You're the one who said accompany you for the weekend. A weekend is more than just a day."

"Hey, I'm not objecting. Maybe you should spend the night."

"Erik--"

"It makes sense. You can really explore the place...or other things," he said, giving me a long look. "Nice dress by the way. Did I already tell you that?"

I knew I was blushing and deliberately ignored his compliment. "Thanks, but no thanks. I won't spend the weekend at your place, but I'll make plans to visit sometime this week. We can discuss it later."

He sighed. "You're missing out. I'm great company.

He meant to say more, I could tell, but suddenly something heading in our direction behind me caught Erik's attention.

That something was actually a someone I quickly found out.

"Erik! Hi! Sorry I'm late," said a cute petite blonde wearing huge sunglasses and not much else. Her shorts were so brief I was scared that if she sneezed I would see her private parts and her top was cropped and barely restraining her gigantic, clearly surgically augmented breasts.

We sized each other up and the instant dislike we took toward each other was readily apparent.

"You were expecting company?" I asked Erik, not bothering to say a word to our new guest. Hmm...I shouldn't have been surprised. If I could be so easily sucked into falling for Erik's charms, plenty of other women probably had too. Maybe Erik was a womanizer. Why was I not surprised?

"As I said, I do like mixing business with pleasure," he said to me with a grin before getting up to greet the young lady who did not look happy to see me.

"Candy, this is Misha, my new interior designer."

"Interior designer. That's not even a real career," she said meanly.

I wanted to punch her in her giant fake boobs, but restrained myself. "Really? And what is it that you do, Candy?"

"It's Candice to you and I'm a pediatric oncologist."

I giggled. "You? Seriously? Really?" Did you get those boobs in med school? Is what I really wanted to ask her.

"What, I can't be fantastically attractive and smart?"

Her nasal voice made me want to cover my ears and scream.

"I wouldn't describe you as either to be honest...first impressions and all," I gave her a nasty smile.

She narrowed her eyes at me and I knew we were going to get into a verbal sparring match when Erik said, "Time out, ladies. You both have your wiles..."

I glared at him and he laughed.

"I'll call you later, Misha. I have some business to attend to now."

"I can only guess what type of business," I said under

my breath as Candy huffily walked out leaving Erik to follow her.

Erik laughed and turned to me. "Not many women make Candy jealous."

I made a gagging face and he laughed again. "I'll call you soon. Thanks for meeting up with me."

He then walked away and as he walked through the door, he glanced back at me and gave me a parting smile.

I couldn't help myself. I smiled back. Clearly, Erik was an outrageous flirt and probably a womanizer if Candy was any indication. I would keep him at arm's length because I really didn't want to get sucked into his form of seduction. I would keep things light and impersonal. After all, I didn't have time to be seduced, I had a life to rebuild. Not to mention, I wasn't interested in being one of many women whose company Erik enjoyed. But, I thought as I gathered my things, I didn't necessarily have to be Erik's conquest...he could be mine. With that intriguing thought, I focused on my design ideas with thoughts of Erik and me in compromising positions on my mind.

A FEW DAYS LATER, I found myself at Erik's house. It was even more breathtaking in person, if not a little grubby.

The previous owner hadn't left it in the best condition. It was going to be a huge undertaking. That made it almost as exciting as the money I would get from taking on the job. Almost.

Erik wasn't there when I arrived. Instead I was greeted by his personal assistant. To my surprise, the personal assistant was a guy named Simon. I thought I was going to meet another bombshell like Candy. Simon was efficient, short, and meticulously dressed. He had a delightful Boston accent and we chatted about being transplants in South Florida.

"I don't miss the cold," he was saying as he took me to the pool house. He opened the door and I looked around.

"I don't miss the cold either, "I said, spinning in a circle, admiring the pool house that was probably 100 times the size of my grandmother's old New York apartment.

"It's impressive, isn't it? I've been trying to convince Erik to let me live in it as part of my benefits package."

I laughed, but apparently it wasn't a joke. "You're serious, aren't you?"

"More serious than a heart attack. I would even take a pay cut to live here."

"It is pretty sweet. Can you imagine being this rich?"

"No, that's why I took this job, so that I could live vicariously through Erik."

"I don't blame you. It sounds like a pretty sweet gig."

He nodded. "It is. Erik pays great. I get days off whenever I feel like it. He's pretty undemanding."

"Funny...I would have figured he'd be the opposite."

"He's pretty easy-going; the only problem I have is screening text messages and phone calls from interested ladies."

Figures, I thought crossly. And then I reminded myself that I didn't care. Erik was just my employer. What he did in his free time wasn't any of my concern.

"So he's pretty popular with the ladies?" I tried to sound nonchalant.

"They won't leave him alone. I guess that's the draw-back of being a billionaire."

Billionaire? I tried not to react to that statement. I'd known just from looking at the property that Erik was loaded, but a billionaire? Wow, I had literally hit the jackpot. A client with unlimited funds! I could make his home look spectacular!

Apparently, Simon realized that he had said too much. He promptly changed the subject and I let my mind wander as he showed me around. There was so much I wanted to do, so many ideas running through my head. I was taking pictures and scribbling notes on my tablet. I was drawing out my ideas and I was feeling energized. And I realized then that not once had I thought of Wyatt or my failed marriage.

I briefly wondered what that meant. Was I finally getting over it? Maybe I was moving on. I didn't get a chance to think about it any longer as I heard footsteps behind us and turned around to see Erik.

He smiled at me and greeted Simon. "I've got it from here...you can take the rest of the day off," he said.

Simon looked surprised. "Are you sure, sir?"

"Very. Get out of here. And stop wearing suits all the time. I keep telling you, you're not my manservant or butler."

Simon looked down sadly at his fashionable and clearly expensive suit and whined, "But it gives me a certain presence, you know what I mean?"

Erik shook his head. "I don't know what you mean, but never mind...wear what you want."

"I'll tone it down," Simon said as if he just had the best idea. "Instead of 3-piece suits, I'll go with that casual jeans and blazer look."

Erik shrugged. "Whatever makes you happy, Simon. I just don't want people thinking I make you dress like a butler."

Simon shook his head. "Big E, you don't have to worry about that. I'm way too young and good-looking to be mistaken for a butler."

"Oh, the arrogance of youth...I miss those days," Erik said, giving me a wink.

"You're arrogant and clearly not youthful, Big E," I quipped.

Simon snickered and then quickly excused himself when Erik shot him an annoyed look.

"Ouch, Misha. You really know how to hit a guy where it hurts. Lots of practice?"

"Just enough," I said with a shrug, giving him a flirtatious smile.

"Sooo...," he said, sitting down on the steps that sat in front of the pool house entrance. "What do you think of the property?"

"It's great. Beautiful."

He nodded in agreement and said as his dark eyes met mine, "I fell in love with this place as soon as I saw it. Love at first sight." He laughed and then his expression became serious. "Do you believe in that?"

"Believe in what?" I said, being deliberately obtuse. Love wasn't a topic I wanted to discuss with him or anyone. Where had love gotten me? Nowhere.

"Love at first sight."

I shook my head, knowing that he was probably playing a game. This was probably something he said to all women.

He surprised me then by saying, "I don't blame you. Neither do I. Now lust though. That's a whole other story."

I narrowed my eyes at him and his smile spread wider.

"You're a shameless flirt. Do you flirt with every woman you meet? If so, that sounds exhausting."

"Exhausting? Exhausting for who?"

"The women. All womankind."

"How dare you judge me? I have standards."

"She has to have a pulse and be between the ages of 18 and 65?"

"How'd you know that?" he joked, acting surprised. "Have you been following me around?"

"You're ridiculous."

"I'm honest," he said with a sexy smile that I couldn't help returning.

He got up and walked near me, coming to stop just in front of me. I held my ground, not stepping back. "I like women. Is that a crime?"

"No...but you could be a little bit more selective...Like, I don't know...have a certain type like most men."

"I'm not most men and why should I restrict myself?"

"There's nothing wrong with a little restriction...you have to set boundaries..."

"Boundaries?" he asked, taking one of my hands in his and pulling me close to him. My body moved toward his on its own accord, enjoying his nearness. His hips pressed against mine and I could plainly feel his sex hard against my thigh.

"Yes, boundaries," I managed to say as my heart raced and my brain ran through a million and one scenarios.

"What are your boundaries now, Misha?"

My mind and body were waging an internal war. Tell him to get lost. Tell him that you're not interested. He's a flirt. A womanizer. A man whore at best...and he was exactly the opposite of my ex. He was everything I needed. At least, at that moment.

He ran his hands up my bare arms bringing me closer as he did. "What are your boundaries?" He repeated softly, bringing his lips down on mine to place a few soft kisses there. They were short, fleeting. And then he made his way to my neck kissing me there, not letting up as he trailed kisses across my collarbone up to just behind my ears. Just behind my ear was my most sensitive spot.

Wyatt hadn't kissed me there in years. Our sex life had become almost robotic. And I didn't know which one of us had been to blame. I liked sex. A lot. And we had had sex often, but it hadn't really been intimate in years. It had just fulfilled a need that both of us had.

I still had those needs and now Erik was going to meet them...at least for now. He led me into the pool house and shut and locked the door.

"Is Simon gone?" I managed to ask before moaning

in pleasure as Erik kissed me again on the lips, this time long and hard.

My nipples hardened too as his hands began to play with my breasts, caressing my nipples until a dull ache began to form between my legs. I shifted a little, as I felt my panties getting wet.

"Simon should be long gone," he said, not bothering to stop his fingers from doing very naughty things to my breasts. He began to unbutton my dress shirt. I had decided to look as professional as possible and still I was being seduced.

Who was I kidding? This was going to happen sooner or later. I was going to be another notch on Erik's bedpost and he was going to be my rebound guy. And I wasn't going to regret it. I deserved a one-night stand. And something about Erik made me sure that his sexual confidence wasn't just an act.

He flung my shirt across the room and quickly rid me of my bra.

He stopped just for a moment to stare at my breasts as he unzipped his pants.

"I don't think I've ever seen such a perfect pair of boobs."

I laughed then, breaking the sexual tension for a moment. I should have expected Erik to be a playful lover.

He shoved his pants down his legs and stepped out of

them and I quickly did the same with my dress pants until we faced each other, me wearing nothing but a thong and him wearing boxer briefs that made me want to rip them off of him and have him take me hard from behind. He was sexy...David Beckham or Mark Wahlberg sexy. His abs were perfectly chiseled and hard. His legs were muscular and his thighs so thick, I felt they could crush me between them. And his arms and chest were taut with muscle.

I wanted him bad. I stepped out of my thong and he did the same with his boxers. His cock wasn't just long, it was also thick. He was significantly bigger than my ex and I wondered if I would be able to comfortably fit him all in.

I didn't get a chance to focus much more on that worry as he pulled me toward him and with a giggle we toppled together onto the couch. I was on top of him and asked him matter-of-factly if he had a condom.

"Yeah," he said in a sexual haze as he reached for his pants that were just almost of out of his reach. He snatched at his pants, found the condom and I did the honors, sliding the condom over his sex, slowly, gripping his penis hard as I stroked the condom over it. I squeezed the tip of his dick and he moaned, slapping me on my butt.

"How do you want it?"

"I don't care. I just want you inside me."

"Damn, you're sexy," was all he said as he brought me underneath him. He parted my thighs with his own and slid into me in one simple motion.

I grunted as his thick sex pushed into me and I struggled to accommodate his length and size.

He began to pump in and out of me and I struggled to get comfortable. He pushed too far in and I gasped in pain.

"You want me to slow down?" he asked.

I nodded, getting turned on by his gentleness. He didn't thrust into me again, he just lay there inside me letting the walls of my sex adjust to the feel of his cock buried deep inside me.

He began to suck my nipples, bringing one into his mouth as he played with the other. The pleasure of his mouth on my nipples made me cry out.

He kissed my mouth then and slid his hand between my legs, slowly parting my folds and beginning to play with the area surrounding my clit. I groaned and began to move my hips so that his sex began to slide in and out of me. He groaned but still didn't move. Instead he focused on my clit, running his finger around the hood over and over, until my movements became frantic as I thrust my hips up over and over, hoping to get him to move inside of me again. I was ready for him now...wet...tight...ready.

He finally got the memo and wrapped my legs

around his waist. My heels dug into his butt as he thrust into me holding on to the edge of the couch as he slid in and out of my wetness, this time being gentle, taking his time.

My thighs began to shake and my hips began to thrust up and down, meeting each of the thrusts that sent me reeling back toward the arm of the couch. I tried to anchor my hands around the cushions, but it was no use. His powerful thrusts had me balled up on the couch, not able to do anything but take the pleasurable thrusts of his cock as it filled me.

I could feel my sex tightening around his cock and he groaned.

"Come for me, Misha," he said as he pulled all the way out and then slowly pushed all the way back in.

I didn't need his permission to come. It was already happening and I felt like my head was about to explode as he took that moment to reach between us and rub my clit as he slowly pushed into me again.

I screamed loudly, shouting his name.

He grabbed my hands and held them above my head, pinning me down as he licked my nipples and thrust shallowly into me, letting just the tip of his penis enter my sex before pulling out and entering just a little more. He was teasing me.

"More," I gasped.

He complied but didn't push all the way in.

"Erik!" I said, frustrated as I attempted to knead his butt with my heels to press him into me.

"Just a little more...I want to feel you come...hang on just a little more..." he said, now thrusting completely into me.

But I was done. My body began to shudder, my head felt like it was about to explode, and an orgasm of the likes of which I'd never felt before hit me. My inner sex shuddered around his dick, clenching and unclenching around it. He groaned and began to ride me hard, I felt myself coming again and again. Wave after wave of pleasure.

I struggled to breathe, to even think as my inner muscles clenched his cock one last time, massaging it with my wetness, sucking him in and trying hard to not let go.

And he came then, gasping for air as my nails dug into his shoulders and I screamed his name.

He immediately rolled off me, seating himself next to me on the floor. He pulled off the condom and tossed it in a waste bin.

"That was---"

"Mind blowing? Hands down the best sex you ever had?"

I laughed as I sat up. "I wouldn't say that..."

"What?" he looked offended. "On a scale from 1 to 10? What was I? An 11?"

"Try seven," I said and he lunged for me and I giggled as he brought me down on the floor on top of him, tickling me.

"Take that back," he said as I rolled around in laughter, trying to evade the fingers threatening to tickle me.

"No! Make me!" I cried, trying to scramble away from him on all fours as I giggled. He scrambled to his knees and caught me.

"A seven, huh?" he said as he pulled my hips back and my butt met his sex. He was becoming aroused again, as he rubbed his cock against my butt. In mere seconds he was hard again. I was breathless in anticipation and greedily stuck my butt in the air, waiting for him to enter me hard from behind. He didn't disappoint, as he quickly sheathed himself in another condom and began to fuck me...this time harder.

He squeezed my tits as he did. Something about being taken by a virtual stranger, on my knees, turned me on and I found myself climaxing quickly. I loved the feel of him inside me. I loved how he took me, claimed my sex as if he owned it. I could get used to this.

And as he came one last time, it was as if he had read my mind. He smacked my butt playfully and mumbled, "A man could get used to this."

5

A few days after my romp in the pool house with Erik, I received a call from Lacey. I was walking around my grandma's condo making sure nothing of value had been left behind. I knew the new owner would be stopping by shortly and I didn't want them to have any complaints about the condition of the property.

I was starting to feel guiltier about Grandma staying with a friend, even though she was clearly enjoying herself. Apartment and condominium pickings weren't exactly slim in South Florida, but affordable pickings were. I couldn't afford 1600 a month for a one-bedroom, but anything cheaper would place her in a community that I didn't feel comfortable leaving her in. It was a conundrum and it was my responsibility to figure it all out. I sincerely hoped I would soon. I just needed a break. Just another streak of luck. And maybe a huge advancement from Erik.

"Girl, I heard you and Erik have gotten awfully cozy and that he invited you out to his place for the weekend," she said gleefully.

"Ugh," I said, feeling sort of put out. I didn't think Erik would be the type to kiss and tell, but apparently I was wrong.

"Don't believe everything you hear." I was being deliberately evasive. I wasn't quite sure how much she knew, but I knew exactly what she would say if she knew the whole story.

"Normally I don't, but I'm so bored, just overhearing juicy gossip gets me excited." She wasn't currently working because she had, once upon a time, been Oliver's personal assistant. In fact, that's how she had met Oliver and eventually Jude. She had told Emmaline and me that she felt it was a little awkward to work for him now that she was not only his daughter-in-law but the mother of his future grandchild, so she had quit. To pass the time until she found another job, she was volunteering at Ophelia's Angels but that was only a couple of times a week. She certainly didn't have to work; between Oliver's fortune and Jude's, Lacey was loaded.

"Well, he did invite me to stay over for the weekend---"

"Ohhhhhhh really---"

"But I declined..." I didn't add that I had spent nearly a whole afternoon having sex with him all over his house.

"Ughh, why do you have to be such a bore?"

"Hey!"

"What?"

"You have always been the uptight one, so don't try to act like you're all adventurous now."

"What? Uptight? Me? Never! I got drunk and married in Vegas, after getting into a fight with someone's bride. I'm not uptight, I'm a Vegas legend."

"That was a fluke. Everyone knows that," I teased. "And word has it that you ran away from that bride so that you wouldn't get beat up and your knight in shining armor ran away too."

She sighed. "I must admit...it wasn't our finest moment."

"Far from it."

"But it was still pretty adventurous...I mean, Misha, you're entitled to...you know... live a little...in the sack," she whispered the last part and I couldn't help but laugh. Lacey was a prude deep down inside. A sexy night in Vegas wasn't going to change any of that.

I wasn't a prude, but for some reason, I didn't want anyone knowing that Erik and I were sexually involved...at least not yet. I didn't know if what happened was just a one-night stand that lasted all day long or if we were going to hook up again. I just knew that I didn't want to be judged for it, not even by my friends. I didn't think Emmaline would approve and if Lacey knew the full details of my agreement with Erik she wouldn't approve either.

We had kind of decided to be friends with benefits and just see where our lust for each other took us. Truth be told, we had spent as much time talking about plans for his house as we did having sex on those plans. I'd never had so much sex in one day. I didn't have much experience with sex outside of marriage, so I wasn't sure if the sexual chemistry between myself and Erik was sustainable, but boy did it make for a good time. I actually woke up a little sore between my legs from all our encounters the day before.

I didn't feel guilty. I didn't feel bad. We were consenting adults and enjoyed pleasuring each other, but that didn't mean I wanted the world to know that I was having sex with my employer.

"How's the baby doing?" I asked, changing the subject.

"Fine. Great. I still have really bad heartburn, but besides that everything's great. She's growing exactly like she's supposed to."

"She!" I asked excitedly, "Did you already find out the sex?"

"Kind of. I mean, we could know, but we've decided

not to ask. We want it to be a surprise. But I just default to she whenever I'm talking about the baby."

"Ohhh okay…are you going to have a gender reveal party when you do want to announce it? They're all the rage nowadays."

"I think they're stupid," Lacey said shortly.

I laughed at her abruptness. "Well, okay…no one's twisting your arm to make you tell us your baby's sex."

"Sorry, I was harsh. I just feel all this pressure to do stuff before the baby's even born. There are a million forums and parenting books. I haven't read one book yet. I find them bossy. Like they're always telling me what I should be eating. What I shouldn't be eating. What I should be doing. What I shouldn't be doing. It's like everyone is trying to tell me what to do and I just wish the world would just shut up and mind its own business." She then started crying suddenly. Just bawling. Uh oh.

"Lacey," I said concerned, "do you need to get away for a little bit?"

"Yes," she said pitifully.

"I'll be right there---"

"No! I'll come to you. Where are you?"

"At Grandma's old condo."

"Okay. I'll get dressed and head out there. I love driving now. It makes me feel in control…and it's like the only control I have left. I'll pick you up in like a half hour and we'll figure out fun stuff to do then. Sound like a deal?"

"Sounds great. I'll see you soon."

We both hung up and I finally thought about how difficult pregnancy must be for my friend. We had been teaching assistants together and while I had enjoyed the kids, I hated the administrative part. Lacey, on the other hand, hated the unpredictability of being around children. She liked controlled environments and preferably she liked to be the one in control.

Not having any control over her body and feeling overwhelmed because of it must be weighing on her, I thought to myself.

Soon enough, she was at my grandma's soon to be ex-condo. I raced down the stairs and hopped in the car with her. As she maneuvered into traffic, I glanced surreptitiously at her. She was still barely showing, but her hair was disordered and her clothes were an odd mix of striped jeans and a tie-dye top that I recognized from an event we went to in college.

"Are you wearing your shirt from that environmental group we were in back in college?"

"Yeah," she said shortly. "Why? Is it wrong to care about the environment after college?"

I held up my hands. "Hey, it was just a question because I recognized the shirt and hadn't seen it in years. Please don't yell at me."

She sighed and to my dismay abruptly crossed two lanes of traffic without signaling, swung the car to the side of the road and pulled over. Cars honked at us and I swear a couple of people gave us the finger.

I was holding onto the dashboard for dear life even though I had on a seatbelt.

"What--" was all I managed to get out before Lacey put her head on the horn and just sobbed, not caring that the pressure of her head made the horn go off incessantly.

I gently placed a hand on her shoulder. "It's okay, Lacey," I said between the sound of the horn and Lacey's sobs. I knew before she even said a word what was going on in her head. I knew Lacey well enough to know she was torturing herself over a situation she couldn't possibly control. "It's going to be okay. You don't have to be perfect. You just have to be you."

Finally, she was able to stop crying and she pulled her head off the steering wheel. Thank god, I thought to myself. I had felt a headache coming on from the constant blaring of the horn.

"I'm sorry," she squeaked, her voice sounded funny from all the crying. "I'm just upset. I hate crying all the time. Do I look ugly? I've always been an ugly crier."

I laughed. I couldn't help myself. "Everyone's ugly when they cry."

"Not true. I bet Heidi Klum is a beautiful crier."

I thought about that for a second and then said, "Yep, you're probably right."

Lacey laughed abruptly. "Oh my god, I'm a mess and I'm going to bring a child into this world. This is crazy." She then turned and looked me in the eye. She seemed so fragile, so young. I think it was because she wasn't wearing makeup and her face was freshly scrubbed. "I'm scared."

Lacey? Scared? Lacey was the go-getter, the bossy one, the one who always took life by the horns. That Lacey was scared? I understood why she was scared, but I couldn't believe she admitted it.

"I haven't told Emmaline because she's so brave and I feel ridiculous being afraid of being a mom when she was so young when she had Dora and she had nothing. I'm married to a billionaire for goodness sake and I'm 31 years old. I have no excuse to be afraid."

I shrugged. "I don't know about that. I think despite any mom's circumstances, she'll be afraid. At least a little...and you shouldn't feel like that about talking to Emmaline. She's your friend, she'll probably be a better comfort to you than someone who has never been pregnant and has no intention of ever being pregnant."

She shook her head. "No, I can't talk to her yet. I'm still too much of a mess."

She sighed deeply before saying, "I was so excited the first few months, but then I started reading expecting mother forums and then my fear factor went from nearly zero to a bajillion."

I couldn't control a giggle. "Stay off the Internet and you'll be fine."

She nodded. "I know you're right...but it's not just that." She seemed reluctant to continue and I frowned.

"Come on, Lacey, you can tell me."

"Well, I just wonder what type of mother I'll be. I don't know much about being a mom. My own mom didn't even stick around to raise me."

I shook my head. My experience as a child made me never want to have children of my own and Lacey's experience as a child made her doubt her ability to raise a child properly. Maybe instead of spending all our money on ice cream, we should have spent it on therapy. I said so and Lacey laughed.

"Naww, that ice cream was a good investment."

We sat there in silence for a little while and then I finally said, "Sorry I couldn't be more helpful."

"It's fine. It's my problem to figure out."

"Yeah, but I'm your friend. I should have had something better to offer besides the trite 'Don't worry. Everything will be okay' response."

"You listened and didn't judge...that's plenty."

We sat there in silence, each of us lost in our own thoughts. "I feel so guilty," Lacey finally said, "so guilty for feeling anything but happy about this pregnancy. So many people are trying for babies and can't get pregnant and all I can think about is how I'm probably the most unfit person to have a baby, and yet I'm pregnant."

"You're not unfit. Never say that again," I said angrily.

"Well, not unfit, just ill-equipped."

I sighed. "No one is the perfect parent and no parent gets everything right. You're being too hard on yourself and you're overthinking it. All you have to do is love her. Or him. That's all that it takes to be a good mom."

She nodded. "You're right." She then turned and hugged me. I held her tight. "Thanks, thanks for listening to my craziness."

"Anytime."

She pulled back and then said with a twinkle in her eye..." So tell me what's going on with you and Erik?"

I sighed. "I thought pregnant women were supposed to be forgetful."

"Pregnancy brain hasn't gotten the best of me yet," Lacey said happily.

"No kidding," I looked at her and asked, "How did you even know?"

"Eavesdropping. I heard Erik and Jude talking and your name came up."

I looked at her with raised brows. "What exactly did you hear?"

"I overheard him asking about you. Like stuff about your divorce."

I groaned. "And what did Jude tell him?"

"Just something about how much of a jerk Wyatt was toward you...I didn't catch the rest of their conversation."

"You're a terrible eavesdropper," I joked, feeling a little vulnerable knowing that Erik had spoken to Jude about me. We were just friends with benefits. Why did he need to know my relationship history? Hmm...interesting.

I heard my phone beep and looked down. It was a text from Erik. I didn't want to look at it just then, especially when I noticed Lacey staring at it. She looked up at me expectantly and gave me a huge smile.

I made a face at her and said, "It's just a text message, Lacey, not a marriage proposal."

She continued to smile as she said, "Not yet, at least." She started her car and pulled safely into traffic. I tried to not visibly seem relieved, but I was nervous for a second there that she might cause an accident. I also found myself thinking about what she said. Marriage was the furthest thing from my mind. I didn't want to get married again, especially not to someone like Erik.

I teased her. "When did you become such a romantic? Trying to pair everyone up."

She shook her head. "You know I'm not a matchmaker, but I don't know, I think it could work between you and Erik."

"There's nothing between me and Erik," I lied, feeling bad about not telling Lacey the truth. But technically, there wasn't...right? It was just sex.

She looked at me briefly and then looked back at the road and shrugged. "If you say so. Speaking of babies...do you think Colin and Emmaline are going to try for another baby?"

I was glad that she changed the subject. "I don't know. That would be great though...both of you pregnant at the same time."

She smiled. "Yeah, I think so too." She gave me a devilish look. "Even if they aren't planning for one, maybe I can convince her."

"Good luck," I laughed.

We decided to go see a movie. It was a romantic comedy and of course, the lead actors eventually got their lives together and ended up with each other. If only life were that simple, I thought to myself. After the movie, Lacey dropped me off at my granny's old condo to get my car. I drove straight over to Oliver's, hiked up to the mansion and went straight to my bedroom in the pool house and sat moodily on my bed. I was feeling sorry for myself. I wasn't silly enough to believe in happily ever after, but some happiness wasn't too much to expect, right?

Emmaline had Colin and Theodora. Lacey had Jude and her soon to be child. And I had a failed business, a failed marriage, and a sex buddy.

I didn't begrudge them their happiness. They deserved it. I just wanted my own life to stop falling apart at the seams.

When I was done feeling sorry for myself, I washed my face and looked for my phone. I found it under my bed.

There was a text from Erik still waiting for me.

"What are you doing?" it simply said.

"Feeling sorry for myself," I mumbled. I tossed the phone across the bed and settled down on my pillow.

My feelings were all over the place. I knew if I were lying to my friends that I was ashamed of my behavior, but who could blame me? I was sleeping with a random guy and I was freshly divorced. I didn't know what to do with my life. I was at a cross path. I was confused and conflicted. It was amazing that I still knew my left from my right.

I decided to just ignore the text message and call my grandma. She didn't answer, so I called my uncle instead. I know they spoke every day.

"Hey, have you heard from Grandma today? I just tried to call her, but she didn't pick up."

"Resting," he said shortly. "She's so stubborn, never

listens to a word I say. She needed a nap. She's got a job and has been working nonstop."

"What? Tell me she's not a driver." I shook my head preparing to hear the worst.

"Worse."

"What's worse than Grandma driving?"

"She works at a call center."

"No!"

"Yep. She's a telemarketer."

I lay back down and placed an arm over my eyes and groaned. "No, no, no, no. My sweet grandmother is harassing people for a living."

"And apparently she's good at it!" Uncle Niko said cheerfully.

"Uncle Niko, don't tell me that." I sat up, forgetting that in all the chaos that had been my life recently, I had forgotten to tell him about Erik's house. "Oh, I've been meaning to tell you, I landed a pretty big gig. Hopefully, it'll lead to other jobs and I'll be able to reopen my business."

"That's great...but make sure that's what you really want."

I looked at the phone. That was strange. What did he mean by that?

"What do you mean by that?"

"I'm just saying maybe you can take this time to get to know yourself. Get to know you better. Find out what you want from life instead of always being what everyone else wants you to be."

"What are you talking about? I wanted to be an interior designer."

"I know...I know, but you were so bent on building an empire because Wyatt did---"

"What! No! I created that business for me...I, I, I wanted it."

"I'm not saying you didn't want it. I'm just saying it became everything to you as if you had something to prove."

"Oh, just stop with the sexist crap. If I had been a man dedicated to my career, you wouldn't be saying these words now, but because I'm a woman suddenly I'm way too dedicated to my career. Give me a break!"

He sighed. "That's not what I'm saying. I'm just saying now you can really focus on making you happy, just you, on your own terms...that could be interior design or being a bum under a bridge. I'm just happy you no longer have to be Misha, Misha's daughter. Or Misha, Kat's granddaughter. Or Misha, Wyatt's wife. You're free to just be you."

For some reason, his words hurt my feelings and I mumbled some excuse about needing to get off the phone.

Is that what he thought of me? That I didn't know who I was unless I was attached to someone else? That really hurt. I always prided myself on being independent. I had launched a successful firm all by myself. I didn't need anyone. Ever. Uncle Niko was wrong.

Determined to get my mind off his ridiculous words, I texted Emmaline to see if she were busy. She was taking Dora to a concert so she was busy. I knew Lacey was still battling her own demon, so that left Erik.

I texted him back, "I'm heading to dinner."

Next thing you know, my phone was ringing.

"Want some company?"

It was Erik.

I didn't know if I wanted company or not now, but hey, I should have just ignored his text or maybe even ignored his call.

I sighed. "I'm not really in the mood."

He paused. "Having a rough day?"

"You could say so."

"Let me help you get over it," his voice was suggestive. I rolled my eyes.

"I'm really not in the mood for THAT."

"Hey, where's your dirty mind wandering off to? I was simply offering you a nice getaway to get your mind off of whatever is bothering you."

I opened my mouth to say no, but couldn't get the words out. I wanted a getaway. I was tired of dealing with my own problems. I just wanted to forget about them for a while.

"What do you have planned?"

"Whatever your heart desires..."

"You really mean that?"

"Do I come across as a liar?"

"Nope. Just a womanizer."

"Valid observation."

I giggled. "Where should I meet you?"

"Walter Cove Yacht Club."

"I'll be there in 20 minutes."

"See you then."

I tossed a swimsuit in my purse, placed my phone on vibrate and jumped into my car.

Fifteen minutes later I pulled up in front of the yacht club. I had a problem with speeding. My problem was that I couldn't stop doing it.

To my surprise, Simon was waiting for me out front.

"Hi there! Come on aboard!"

I gave Simon a big smile and followed him. I spotted Erik moving toward us. Instantly my heart began to race and my skin flushed. This was bad. My body reacted to just seeing him as if he were my favorite drug. God, I hoped Erik didn't become my addiction. I made myself look away from him as he approached. He was trouble. Yep, I thought when our eyes met, I was in for some trouble.

6

____

"I can handle it from here," Erik said to Simon, who looked at him annoyed.

"I'm running out of things to do," Simon whined.

"Really, Simon?" asked Erik incredulously. "Are you complaining because I'm giving you the day off?"

"My aunt and uncle are in town," he said with a long-suffering sigh. "They're from Idaho or Utah...maybe North Dakota, I don't know. All I know is that they're driving me crazy."

"Go home to your family. Deal with it like the rest of us."

"You're lucky you're an orphan," Simon mumbled before leaving.

I turned to Erik. "He's kind of bitter, isn't he?"

He shrugged. "Simon's always been a little rough around the edges."

As we were walking along, I couldn't help but ask, "Are you really an orphan?"

He chuckled. "I wish."

"What's that supposed to mean?"

"It just means life would have been easier if I were."

I waited for him to explain further, but he didn't. I shrugged it off. We all had our secrets; Erik was entitled to his.

"So what's the plan for today?"

"A trip on my yacht."

"Lead the way."

"I hope you brought your swimsuit."

"Yep, you got yours?"

"Nope. I figured I'll give you something good to look at and go commando."

"I feel my eyes burning already."

"Is that your way of calling me hot? Because if so, you're right."

I had to laugh. He didn't come across as arrogant, just self-confident. And I liked that.

He led me to his yacht which I'm sure was several million dollars. I was introduced to the ship's captain and then Erik took me downstairs.

I changed into my swimsuit and he changed into his trunks and we made our way to the front of the ship. We sat in lounge chairs and a bottle of champagne sat in a bucket of ice between us.

"So tell me about yourself, Misha. Let's turn the tables a little bit. I want to know more about you. What makes you tick?"

"You know enough already."

"I want to know more." I could tell from his tone that he meant it.

I cleared my throat. "Let's see what you don't already know. I was raised by my grandmother. I was dumped by my husband."

"His loss."

"I agree. Your turn."

"I wasn't raised by anyone."

"But you must have come from somewhere?"

"My mom abandoned me when I was a kid..."

"How old?"

"About seven."

"I'm sorry."

"So am I...I spent my formative years in various foster homes. It went from bad to worse until finally I said screw it and left."

"How old were you when you decided to walk out on your own?"

"Fourteen."

"You were just a baby," I said, even though I had been around the same age when I walked away from my parents' home.

"I'd felt that I'd lived a thousand years by that time."

Something about his tone told me those years had been rough. I didn't want to get into it. It was clearly a painful subject for him. If it wasn't, he wouldn't have avoided talking about it for so long.

"How did you meet Oliver?" I asked instead.

"Like I mentioned, I tried to rob him. I tried to steal his phone when he was in McDonald's."

I didn't know what I was most surprised about, that Oliver had eaten at McDonald's or that Erik had been a teenage criminal.

"So what happened when you tried to steal his phone?"

"He swatted me over the head with a bag full of fries and burgers."

I laughed so hard, I almost fell out of my chair.

"He really got my attention."

I laughed again.

"The people at McDonald's called the cops on me. The cops were going to take me away when Oliver intervened, said he wouldn't press charges. He showed up the next day at my foster home. I didn't know how he tracked me down."

"One of the advantages of being a billionaire, I'm sure."

Erik nodded. "I was shocked to see him. I thought he was there to press charges even though he had said that he wouldn't. Growing up the way I did meant I didn't trust anyone…least of all adults. But he was there to help me. I didn't believe him or want his help at first, but he was persistent. He was determined to save me from myself."

He chuckled dryly. "I made his life a living hell, but he stuck with me anyway. Eventually, he even helped me get placed with a better family. If it wasn't for him, who knows where I might have ended up. I owe a lot to Oliver. He became my guardian ad litem. He spoke for me in court. He was the only permanent person in my life."

"How did Jude take that?" I was curious because I knew Oliver and Jude never really saw eye to eye.

"Honestly, he was pretty cool about it. It kept his dad distracted so he wasn't always breathing down his throat."

"Knowing Oliver, I can see how that could be a good thing."

Erik chuckled. "Oliver's, well, he's Oliver, but I probably owe all my success to him."

We were both quiet for a while, lost in our own thoughts.

Finally, Erik turned to me and said, "Now that we know each other's stories, can we jump into the sack?"

"I thought you'd never ask."

He took my hand and pulled me toward him. He surprised me then by picking me up and wrapping my legs around his waist. I wrapped my arms around his neck and kissed him deeply. Our lips stayed locked together as we stumbled toward his luxurious bedroom. Minutes later we fell back to the bed breathing heavily. Our encounter had been quick, yet satisfying.

"Owww..." I groaned, rubbing at my thigh.

"What's wrong?" Erik asked, lifting up on his elbow.

"Too much activity...and awkward angles. I didn't know I had to be a gymnast or body contortionist to be able to sleep with you."

"Body contortionists are sexy."

"Maybe you should date one of them instead."

"So is that what we're doing? Dating?"

"That's not what I would call it."

"Friends with benefits then?"

"Exactly."

He received a call then and he kissed me soundly on the lips before answering. "I have to take this. But I like the friends with benefits idea, because I don't do relationships."

"I wouldn't be interested in one even if you were offering."

"Finally, a woman who won't stalk me."

"That's 100 percent guaranteed."

He walked away to talk on his phone. A few seconds later, I could hear him speaking. He sounded angry, I thought to myself as he raised his voice. When he came back, he didn't say a word to me. He just poured himself a shot and then slammed it back.

"Everything okay?" In the short time that I'd known Erik, I'd never seen him visibly upset.

"No."

"Want to talk about it?"

"Nope." He took another drink and sat down heavily on the couch. I came over and sat next to him, folding my legs under me.

"I'm just going to stare at you awkwardly until you tell me what's wrong."

"You'll be staring for years then," he said, rubbing his face forlornly.

"Come on, Erik. It can't be that bad."

He shook his head. "Let's not talk about this. It's boring. Come here."

He picked me up and brought me into his arms. I settled into them, enjoying the feel of him holding me. He wasted no time as he stuck his hand under the night shirt that he had graciously given me, fondling my breasts with his large warm hands.

He then began to kiss my neck, pulling my shirt up and off me as he did. He let it hit the floor and rolled on top of me and raised my hands up, pinning my hands in place as he traced kisses down my sternum, stopping to suck my nipples. He kept going lower, placing kisses across my belly, licking my belly button and making me giggle.

But as his mouth went lower, I sucked in a breath in anticipation. The playfulness was gone; it was go time. He slowly parted my folds and began licking me up and down, penetrating and tasting me with his tongue. I stirred my hips against his mouth and began to moan. He released my hands and I used them to grip his head, holding his head there between my legs, not wanting his mouth to stop the exquisite pleasure it was giving.

He began to finger me then, pushing one finger and then two deep inside me. My legs began to shake and I wrapped them around his back. I came then, hard, shaking as I bucked against him. He gave my clit one last lick and sat up.

He looked for a condom and, frustrated, found one. He quickly put it on and brought my legs around his hips. He entered me easily. I held on to the couch as I rode him. He spread my thighs further apart and pushed into me.

I groaned as his thick, hard heat filled me.

"You're so tight," he moaned as he pushed into me slowly and pulled out even slower. I protested each time he pulled out. I wanted him to stay there, buried deep inside me. I realized at that moment, the only thing I was sure of was that Erik gave me pleasure. The sex. The hotness. It was all selfish want being fulfilled. Lust. And at that moment in my life, lust was what I could handle.

I don't know which one of us came first. But after that romp, we did it again. Moving from the couch to the floor. We were like horny teenagers and finally as night began to fall, we fell breathless onto his large bed.

He curled up around me and stroked my hair.

"You always smell like strawberries to me."

"Strawberry shampoo," I replied simply.

"I think of you every time I drink a smoothie."

I laughed hard. I liked being around Erik. He was so carefree, so easy to be around. While Wyatt had always been really intense and focused, Erik was the opposite. I didn't understand how I could be so attracted to a man who was the very opposite end of the spectrum to what I was used to. I needed to stop comparing apples to oranges, I thought to myself.

"So are you going to tell me what's bothering you now or are we going to have sex again until our brains stop functioning?"

"I like that idea," he said, running his hand up the side of my hip.

I smiled brightly at him and playfully slapped his hand away.

"Come on, tell me what's going on. We're friends. Sex buddies. Come on, Erik. You've seen all my stuff."

"You've seen all mine too."

I laughed. "What I'm trying to say is that I think it'll be okay to be a little vulnerable with each other. I promise you, I won't make you marry me just because you tell me your problems."

He looked at me with a frown, "Are you sure?"

I punched him in the arm. "Spill it."

He paused and his face became serious. "I'm looking for a surrogate."

"A surrogate?" Of all the things I expected him to say, something about a surrogate was the last thing I had expected. I had thought he was going to say something about work. After all, he was a billionaire. Didn't they work all the time?

"I've always wanted to be a father and have a family. And a surrogate will help make that happen."

I didn't know much about being a surrogate and I didn't know what to say.

He got up from the bed and walked away from me. He leaned against his dresser and said with a frustrated sigh, "I can't believe this."

"What exactly happened with the surrogate? Did she back out or something?"

He nodded. "I had what I thought was the perfect surrogate and she backed out at the last minute. Something about her ex-husband coming back into the picture and now they want to try to have another kid of their own."

I didn't think for a second the same would happen with Wyatt and me.

"You'll find someone else," I said, not knowing what else to say.

"It's a long drawn out process. I've been waiting 5 months for the agency to place me with someone...and now this! I'm pissed."

"Maybe you can expand your search...try another agency."

"Can't. I signed a contract with this one."

"A contract? Surrogacy is a serious business."

"You have no idea."

"So what made you decide to get a surrogate?"

"Like I said. I wanted a child, so a surrogate seemed the way to go."

"There are other ways to, ummm...get a kid. Do I need to explain the birds and the bees to you?"

He scoffed. "You're hilarious." He then sat back down and said, "I don't like complications. I don't like relationships. Getting someone pregnant the "natural way" wouldn't be very conducive to my current lifestyle."

"Ugghh...you make it sound so clinical."

"The surrogate process is a clinical process...which is what I find so attractive about it."

"I've never wanted kids," I admitted, "so I don't get what's so attractive about any of it, being a surrogate especially sounds sucky. Like you carry someone's baby for 9 months and you don't even get to keep it afterward? Sounds like it would be a very emotionally charged situation."

"That's why it takes a special person to be a surrogate. Not to mention, I'm paying the person $50,000 per trimester."

My eyes widened. "How many trimesters are women pregnant?"

He laughed. "I feel like that's something you should know...given that you're a woman and all."

"Like I said, kids weren't ever on my radar so I don't even know."

"Is that part of the reason things ended between you and your ex?"

I looked at him. "Now things are getting personal, I see."

He shrugged. "You don't have to answer that if you don't want to."

"No, it's okay. He cheated. Got another woman pregnant and dumped me."

"Sounds like a real winner."

"I thought he was. I thought I was doing really good for myself by marrying him. I couldn't have been more wrong."

"We all make mistakes. Trust the wrong people."

Curious, I said, "Who did you trust?"

"My ex-wife."

I was shocked. "You were married before?"

"Well, clearly...since I have an ex-wife and all."

"You know what I mean. Tell me everything. What was she? A model, astronaut, brain surgeon?"

He laughed. "For the record, Candy is not my ex-wife and she is just a friend. She was helping me interview pediatricians. Not that that's happening anymore."

"That's a thing? Interviewing pediatricians before the kid even pops out?"

He nodded. "I have a whole list of things I need to do."

"Woah, parenting in 2017 sounds intimidating."

"It is."

"And yet, you want to do it."

He shrugged. "I never really had a functional family of my own, but that's never stopped me from wanting to be a father."

"Did you consider adopting?"

He nodded. "Definitely, and I plan to someday...but maybe now is some day since I don't know when I'll have another surrogate lined up."

"Well, I think adoption is a great option, but you shouldn't give up on your surrogate plan. Just be patient."

He started pacing, clearly frustrated. "I'm sick of being patient."

I didn't know what else to say. And I sensed that Erik might want to be alone tonight.

"I think I should be leaving…"

He walked toward me and pulled me into his arms. "I want you to stay, but I'll probably ruin the rest of our night by being moody and angry."

"I get it," I said, slowly pulling away from his warmth. "Everyone needs a little space sometimes. We'll catch up later this week."

He surprised me by kissing my cheek and trailing a hand through my hair. He tilted my chin up to look in my eyes. "Sorry for messing up tonight."

"Don't apologize. I'm a wild sleeper anyway…I probably would have kicked you in the face or something."

"I value my teeth, so maybe it's best if you never spend the night."

"Hey!"

He hugged me close to him and placed his chin on top of my head. "I'm joking. Just joking. Tonight's out, but some other night…maybe."

"Maybe," I replied. He kissed me again and let me go. I dressed silently and as I was leaving, I said, "Try to get some sleep tonight. Maybe things will be different in the morning."

"You're an optimist."

"Actually, no, just a realist. People change their minds

all the time. Maybe your surrogate will realize she actually doesn't want to get back together with her ex."

"Maybe, but if that's what makes her happy...I can't really begrudge her that."

He looked sad and I touched his shoulder one last time. "You're a good guy, Erik."

He shrugged. "I do my best."

I walked away and he grabbed my hand. I looked into his eyes, filled with raw emotions. This was hitting him harder than he wanted me to know.

"What is it?" I asked.

"Just thanks. Thanks for being here...thanks for listening."

I shrugged. "That's what friends are for, right?" I stood on my tippy toes, kissed his mouth and made my way off his yacht. When I looked back he was watching me from the lounge area. I waved to him and he waved back before disappearing back into his room.

I drove away that night feeling contemplative. First Wyatt and now Erik. Both men were forming a family. And again, I was the odd woman out. It made me feel deficient for some reason that I couldn't quite figure out. I almost felt defective, for lack of a better word, and conflicted. Children weren't for me. Right? Then why did I find myself questioning my wants and desires...especially when it came to Erik? Why was I jealous of a surrogate that I'd never met? I hadn't been jealous of

Wyatt's lover. I didn't even know or care to know her name. I guess it all came down to the fact that deep down, I wanted Erik to want more. Or maybe I wanted more with Erik. Yes, we were developing a relationship, a friendship of sorts. But we were just friends with benefits, right? Then why when he let me go did my body instantly miss him? His warmth?

That's all physical, Misha. All physical. It's just sex, I told myself. Then why was I so upset when he took my hand, but still let me go?

PART II

7

I had agreed to meet Erik for a run. It had become our Monday routine. And it normally led to us ripping each other's clothes off and having sex in the shower. I was thinking that I was due for a bikini wax when someone smacked me on the butt.

"Ouch!"

"Sorry, I couldn't help myself."

"Whatever, that's a lie. You have plenty of self-control."

"Not when it comes to you," he said teasingly. Something about his tone gave me pause. He sounded sincere.

And as I looked up at him, he looked back at me. Our eyes connected and the usual heat between us was replaced by something else.

I looked away first, not knowing how to react, not knowing what to say. I had to be careful, something about our relationship was changing and I didn't know how I felt about that. We had been seeing each other for a couple of months now. He hadn't mentioned his surrogate again and something about the way he avoided the subject completely made me too wary of what his response would be if I asked about it.

Even though I was working for him, I felt we spent an inordinate amount of time together. It was my fault really. I always needed his opinion on something in the house. And he always stopped whatever he was doing to answer me.

We sort of drifted into a routine that felt suspiciously like dating, but I wasn't going to define our relationship if he wasn't interested in doing the same. So I played it cool and pretended that I was okay with the way things were going, even though I kind of wasn't. I think I was falling for Erik, whether I liked it or not. And all of me wondered if Erik maybe felt the same way.

"Shall we?" he asked.

A creature of habit, he set the pace as usual and I easily stayed with him. I was so lost in thought that I didn't see the puddle in front of me and instead of leaping over it, I stepped right into it, slightly off balance.

I flew forward and hit the ground. My knees took most of the brunt of my fall and before I could even contemplate the pain, Erik was there lifting me up.

"Are you okay? Why were you trying to beat up the ground?"

I smiled despite the pain I was in. "Shut up and just help me to the car."

He wound an arm around my waist and gently guided me to the car. I was limping along when suddenly he picked me up as if I weighed close to nothing.

I instantly tensed up. "Put me down."

"No."

I started squirming, pushing at his arms.

"Put me down before you drop me," I said, still trying to get free. I was a little self-conscious about my weight and I didn't really want anyone knowing that I had bones of steel...at least that's what I told the doctor every time I stepped on the scale.

"The only way I'll drop you is if you keep squirming."

"Well, I'm going to keep squirming until you put me down."

"Fine," he said, sounding frustrated.

He found the nearest park bench and deposited me on it. My butt hit the bench with a thud and I looked up at him full glare.

"Don't look at me like that. You need to learn to accept help every now and then."

"I didn't need any help. I was happily limping along."

"Limping is the operative word there. I was worried that you were doing further damage."

"The only way I would have been damaged is if you dropped me any harder on my butt," I said rubbing it. "I'm probably going to have a bruise tomorrow."

"Here, let me rub it. Sorry for dropping you so hard." He moved to rub my butt and I hit at his hand.

"We're in public!" I screeched.

He shrugged. "So what?" He reached to rub my butt again and I hit at his hand again.

"Just help me up. Can you do that at least?"

"Only if you stop snapping at me."

"I'll stop snapping at you if you stop messing things up."

"So trying to help you is messing things up?"

"Yes," I said meanly.

He looked like he wanted to say more, but instead he shook his head and reached for my hands. I let him take them this time as he gently pulled me up.

"Sorry, my caveman instincts kicked in...we must have looked pretty ridiculous just now."

"Yep."

He gave me an apologetic smile. "How about I just walk close to you and if you seem to be about to fall over, I'll catch you."

I smiled back at him. "Now that's what I call a plan."

I limped back to the car under the watchful gaze of

Erik. And I'm not over exaggerating how watchful he was. It was as if he felt I would break at any moment.

"I'm not a porcelain doll," I joked.

"What?" he said, clearly not understanding.

"You're watching me as if you think I'll break."

I reached out for his hand and squeezed it. "I'm fine, okay?"

He studied me. "When you fell, it looked really painful."

"It was painful, but I'll just walk it out...isn't that what most professional athletes do?"

"Well, um, yeah, but you're not a professional athlete."

I nodded. "Another good point."

We fell back into silence until we got back to the car and it was then that I noticed that our hands were still entwined.

Slowly, we pulled away from each other. We didn't say a word as we stood under the now illuminating street lights.

"Well, this night didn't go as planned."

"Nope."

"Want to get tacos?"

"I need to get some work done. I don't really have the time---"

"But you work for me..."

"So..."

"Well, I demand that you take the rest of the day off."

"Errr...it doesn't work quite like that."

"It does now." He walked forward until he was just an inch away from me. He bent down and kissed my forehead, surprising me.

"Be good. If you won't have tacos with me, at least get some rest. And charge me for it."

I smiled wide. "Now that's a good idea."

"I'm full of good ideas."

"No," I said, shaking my head, "actually you're not."

He swatted me on the butt again and said, "Get out of here, before I kidnap you. See you later."

He walked away from me then and I watched him, feeling conflicted. Was I really starting to develop feelings for Erik, but most importantly, was he starting to develop feelings for me?

I watched him get into his car and then I promptly got into mine. I drove without really thinking to the pharmacy. My mind was on Erik the whole time.

I could feel that the nature of our relationship was changing, but I had ignored it. And now things were getting complicated and I didn't know what I wanted to do. I wasn't interested in a relationship. Okay, that's a lie. I was lying to myself. I definitely wanted a relationship with Erik. But was he interested? Didn't he say he didn't do relationships?

And what if he decided to change his mind? What if

he asked me to be in a relationship with him? Would I really say no?

I walked around aimlessly for a few minutes and then decided to just ask the cashier where the painkillers were. She was a blotchy teen and moodily pointed toward the sign that clearly said painkillers.

"Oh, there's a sign. Sorry."

I could tell it took the teenager's every ounce of self-control to not roll her eyes at me.

I chuckled to myself and limped toward the painkiller aisle. And I stopped dead in my tracks.

My throat closed up when I saw him and I wanted to immediately run out and disappear. But whatever, I wasn't the type to back down and run, so I figured I shouldn't start now. And let's be honest, I couldn't run in my present shape anyway.

So with as much dignity as I could muster, I squared my shoulders and made my way toward the painkillers where my ex-husband was currently standing, facing me, but still looking down at the box of pills in his hand.

He hadn't spotted me yet, but I knew in a few seconds he would.

I counted down in my head. Five, four, three, two---

He began walking toward me without even looking up. "Misha!" he said, surprised as he almost plowed into me.

"Hello, Wyatt. Excuse me," I said, not even giving him

another glance as I studied the bajillion bottles of painkillers in front of me. I rarely took meds, so I didn't know what I was doing or what to buy. I only knew that I didn't want to be in any more pain and my knee and ankle were killing me.

"So, hi...how are you?" he said to the back of my head.

I didn't bother turning around as I replied, "Great." I didn't ask him how he was doing. Why would I? I could only hope the painkillers were for his balls because someone had punched him there.

If only my thoughts could manifest into reality, I thought wistfully to myself.

"I see you scratched up your knee. Want me to take a look at it?"

Annoyed, I said, "I didn't know you were still here. And no, I don't want you to take a look at it. Being an engineer does not mean you're an MD. Just FYI."

"Still my fiery Misha."

I turned and looked at him. "First of all, I'm not yours. The divorce was finalized almost five months ago. And second of all, why are you still here?"

"There's no need for so much animosity--"

"You stuck your penis into another woman's vagina," I said matter-of-factly. "I think I'm entitled to treat you with as much animosity as I can muster."

I didn't wait for him to reply, as I looked around him

and continued to study the painkillers available. Maybe I'll just ask the pharmacist...I thought to myself. I realized then that I was practically looking through Wyatt...and the strange part was...I felt nothing.

I no longer felt anything. In fact, I think the original nervousness I felt had nothing to do with him and all to do with not knowing how this moment was going to play out. I was never afraid of confrontation, but I hadn't wanted to get into it in the middle of Walgreens with my ex either.

I finally really looked at him as I made a selection and noticed that he was standing directly in front of me waiting for me to say something. Wyatt looked good, I grudgingly admitted. His bloat from too many carbs and not enough exercise was replaced by a more trimmed body. Maybe his mistress made him work out. One had to look good for one's mistress, I supposed.

His appearance wasn't the only thing that was different. He seemed calmer, more relaxed. It appeared that he was happy. Great. Just great. Truth be told, I wanted him to be miserable. Very miserable. He had made me so miserable in my heart, he deserved any and all the misery the world had to offer.

I guess karma hadn't caught up with this new, improved version of Wyatt. Damn, I hated karma.

"So how are you?" he asked, clearly not intending to move. Great. So I was going to have to actually have a conversation with him. I wasn't having a very good day. First, I mess up my ankle and clobber my knee, next I can't deal with my feelings for Erik, no matter what they might be, and now my cheating, philandering, granny kicking out ex wanted to chitchat. No, thank you.

"Fine. Would you excuse me? I'm sort of in a rush and I didn't come here to chitchat."

He looked disappointed and blurted out, "It wasn't mine."

"What?" I asked, very confused.

"The baby..."

I frowned. What the hell was he talking about? And then it hit me and I couldn't stop the smirk that crossed my face. "You mean the love child?"

He blushed and looked down at his shoes. He was ashamed to meet my eyes. Good, I thought.

"Jenna, well, she was cheating on me...she told me right after I ended it with you that the baby wasn't mine."

I smiled. Karma had done her job. Yay, karma!

"So let me get this right...you were being cheated on by the person you were cheating with?"

He finally raised his eyes, looked me dead in the eye and nodded.

"Sucks to be you," I said succinctly and moved to get into the long line that was now forming at the register. Where had all these people come from? Was it some sort of law of the universe that as soon as you're ready to check out everyone else is too?

I sighed and got in line. Unfortunately, Wyatt followed me there. "So how have you been? Are you seeing someone?"

"That's none of your business."

"Yeah, you're right." He looked dejected. Maybe I was being petty, but his dejected look made me feel great.

"Listen, I'm really sorry---"

"Sorry for what? That you cheated on me? Sorry that your mistress dumped you is more like it."

He shook his head. "No, I'm sorry that I hurt you. I should have ended it between us a long time ago."

I was confused. "By us do you mean me and you or you and Jennifer?"

"Jenna."

I rolled my eyes. "Whatever...Jennifer, Jenna, all the same to me. Anyway, I don't particularly care for this conversation, Wyatt. I'd rather not discuss all my business in front a bunch of strangers in Walgreens. I don't think that's too unreasonable."

He nodded and looked around as if he was finally noticing the people ahead of us and behind us. "You're right. Maybe we can talk elsewhere? Maybe over coffee?"

"Over coffee? What the hell is wrong with you? You

really think I have nothing better to do than sit around chatting with my loser ex?"

I had gotten loud and several people had turned around to stare at us. Wyatt looked ready to hide in a hole now. "Well, I---"

I held up my hand. "Stop. Just stop talking. I don't want to hear anything you have to say. And nothing you will say will make up for how you betrayed me, how you hurt me," I whispered harshly. "And," I said, restraining myself from clobbering him with the bottle in my hand, "it was really low of you to throw my grandma out."

He looked pained. "Yeah, I was an ass. I did that on purpose to hurt you. I was just angry because I thought the judge was going to award you the house."

"You're a real winner," I said, thinking of Erik's assessment of Wyatt. He was so right. "You would have thought that after 8 years of marriage I would have known how ugly a person you are."

He looked ashamed again and said, almost pleadingly, "If I could rewind time, I would. I wouldn't have taken away your granny's home."

"It's fine. We don't want your charity nor do we need it." Thanks to the job I took with Erik I had been able to get my grandma another place to stay. She had actually preferred to stay at the home with her friend, so even though there was a long waiting list, I was able to jump on the first opening there. It was a small studio apartment, not much bigger than a hotel room, but it was in the heart of the city and Grandma thought it was perfect. She was surrounded by seniors and more active than she had been in years. Not to mention, she still insisted on working. She told me it was like getting paid to chitchat except that a lot of people hung up on you or yelled. I loved my granny.

"I know---I wasn't offering charity---I mean I should---God, I'm messing this all up," he shook his head and said, "I'm just sorry. For everything."

I had dreamt of this day when Wyatt came back to me apologizing for his foolish ways. Strangely enough, in my dream I was always on Mt. Olympus dressed like Athena, while Wyatt groveled in front of me, pleading with me to not turn him into a jackass.

In my dream I always laughed wickedly, pointed a staff at him and turned him into a buck-tooth donkey. Reality wasn't nearly as much fun or impressive as my dreams. We were in Walgreens for god's sake, in line with a bunch of strangers while I stood around not in a goddess-like gown but in a pair of shorts and a sports bra with a busted-up knee.

Speaking of which, my knee was starting to burn. I was next in line and turned to Wyatt and said, "This has been fun. Let's not do this ever again. Good luck with life. Buh-bye."

He looked like he wanted to say more, but he was

smart and didn't. He turned away from me without another word and made his way out of the door. Immediately the alarm sounded and he rushed back in, eyes wide.

"I forgot this was in my hand. I'm so sorry," he said, passing a bottle of painkillers to the cashier who looked bored and not the least worried that a customer had technically stolen something.

"You should have him arrested," I said to the cashier who just shrugged her shoulders.

"Whatever. That would be way too much work. That'll be 8 dollars," she said as she tossed Wyatt's pills behind her without even looking and finished ringing me up.

I looked at her, looked at the little box of pills and said, "Seriously? Almost ten dollars for this little bottle of pills?"

"I don't make the rules, I just sell the drugs," she said with a little laugh. Apparently, she was attempting to be witty and clever. If she hadn't been so useless earlier, I probably would have been more inclined to laugh at her little joke.

I paid the eight dollars, albeit bitterly, and limped with my pills back to my car, the whole time cursing the pharmaceutical industry for the price of pills.

As I lowered myself gently into the driver's seat, I thought about the day I'd had. And at the end of the day, it wasn't my ex I was thinking of, it was Erik. Wyatt had barely been a blip on my radar.

I was surprised. Eight years of marriage and I felt nothing for him.

I picked up the phone and dialed Emmaline and Lacey. They both picked up and I told them all that happened. I ended by saying how I was indifferent to Wyatt.

"I can't say that I'm surprised," said Lacey first.

"Me neither," Emmaline chimed in.

"You guys just seemed to be going through the motions for years. I'm kind of surprised you weren't divorced sooner," Lacey said.

"What?!" This was news to me. I had no idea my friends felt that way.

"Come on now, Misha. You must have known Wyatt wasn't the right guy for you."

"No," I said softly, "I didn't know that. Why didn't you guys tell me?" My voice broke and I instantly pulled the car over, not wanting to cry while on the road.

I was able to hold back the tears, but my sadness was quickly replaced with anger.

"Why didn't either of you say anything?"

"It really wasn't our place to say anything," said Emmaline. "I mean, Wyatt wasn't a bad guy and he treated you great---"

"Aside from the cheating--" Lacey cut in.

"Yeah, aside from that," Emmaline added.

A terrible thought occurred to me and I just had to ask. "Wait. Did you guys know he was cheating?"

"No!" they shouted simultaneously.

I believed them. "We totally would have told you if we had found out he was cheating."

Emmaline added, "It would have been all over the news because we would have jumped him and his mistress if we had caught them in action."

I knew they were being sincere. "Well, I'm glad you guys didn't have to get involved in the mess I called a relationship."

"But maybe we should have said something? I don't know. None of us really grew up knowing what a functional marriage looked like," Lacey said.

She was right. Lacey was raised by her single aunt and didn't really know her parents. Emmaline had been estranged from her parents until recently and then there was me, emancipated at the age of 16 and living with my grandmother. Clearly, we were also survivors...like that Destiny Child's song. I wondered which one of us was Beyoncé then, hopefully me.

I knew I was delirious from the pain then since I was comparing myself to a gorgeous pop singer.

As we said our goodbyes, I hung up even more confused than I started. I felt as if everyone had known I had been living a charade, but they had been too chicken to tell me. I felt like a fraud. I had thought my marriage was working. Isn't that why I stayed with Wyatt? I had loved him, right? Hadn't I? Now I couldn't be too sure.

Had I married him for security or because I thought I loved him? I had thought marrying him had been the right thing to do. Now I wasn't so sure anymore.

And if I was unsure of how I felt about my husband of eight years then could I really trust how I was starting to feel about Erik? Did I really care for him or was I just replacing one guy with another? Was that what I was doing, swapping one set of problems for another?

Maybe that was my specialty, finding men that couldn't emotionally commit. Isn't that what Wyatt and Erik had in common? Otherwise they were like night and day.

But did it actually matter? Because at the end of the day, all I would ever be to Erik was a friend and the occasional lover. He wasn't looking for anything real or long-term.

And neither was I. At least, that's what I was going to tell myself to get through another lonely night.

8

____

"Any luck finding a surrogate?" Oliver asked Erik abruptly. I looked at Erik, also wanting to know. It had been weeks or maybe months since the night he had received the phone call telling him that his surrogate was backing out. We hadn't talked about it since.

He shook his head and kept on eating.

"Why not just ask Misha? She needs the money and she's healthy, baby-making age."

I began to choke on my bagel and Lacey offered me a glass of water. We were all sitting out on the balcony that was situated toward the back of the house over-looking the expansive pool. Just one of the perks of living in a mansion, I thought to myself.

"Healthy, baby-making age? What is that even supposed to mean?" I asked Oliver. I was accustomed to

130

his randomness, but even this was a little bit much for me.

"Don't be crass, Dad," Jude hissed at him.

"If I weren't crass, then I wouldn't be me," Oliver replied unrepentantly.

"And you wonder where Jude gets it from," Lacey said, rubbing her expansive belly and smiling.

Oliver laughed. "I don't wonder. I know."

I had agreed to join them for dinner, but I hadn't expected Erik's surrogate to be the topic of conversation. I felt so uncomfortable, I started stuffing myself with whatever was in front of me.

"Just imagine how great it would be to be pregnant together," Lacey said, still rubbing her belly.

I shook my head. "That sounds like the opposite of a good time."

Erik cleared his throat, wiped his mouth with a cloth napkin and said, "Oliver, we've been over this before. I'm not interested in talking about it again."

Oliver looked taken back. "Are you reprimanding me?"

"Sounds like he is," Jude said smiling at Erik. "It's about time someone did. You get away with way too much. Always trying to tell other people how to live their lives."

"I'm not trying to be controlling. I'm just trying to help Erik get the family he deserves. I'm sure he wants more than just you as his surrogate brother," Oliver said sharply to Jude.

"I don't know," Erik said teasingly. "Jude is pretty awesome. Maybe I'll just adopt him instead."

"I'll gladly give him up," Jude and Oliver said at the same time pointing at each other.

We all laughed gleefully.

"Listen, Misha and I need to get back to my house. We have an order coming out shortly."

I looked at Erik curiously. What was he talking about?

"Fine, go. Abandon an old man. If you don't want to talk about the surrogate stuff just say so, but don't leave me with these two." He gestured toward Lacey and Jude who were no longer paying attention to the conversation going on around them. They were both staring at Lacey's tummy and to my surprise I could see it moving.

"Lacey," I whispered, "your belly is moving."

"I know. The baby's kicking. Want to feel?"

I shook my head. "No. What if I press too hard and hurt something? No, I'll just stay here and look from afar."

We all watched in awe for a few minutes and then Erik caught my eye and mouthed, "Let's get out of here."

I nodded and stood up. I reached over Jude and gave Lacey a hug. "We're heading out. See you later."

Oliver didn't look happy, but grumbled a goodbye to

both of us, before shouting once we reached the door, "Just consider my idea! It might just work!"

* * *

"Oliver can be so pushy."

"Tell me about it," Erik said as we sat in his car.

"Your place or mine?"

"Mine," I said, referring to my new apartment not too far from my granny's place. I wanted to be sure to be no more than ten minutes from her in case she needed me.

"I have a client I need to meet with in the morning."

He glanced away from the traffic to look at me and then looked back at the road. "You didn't tell me you landed another client."

"I went to a trade show armed with pictures of what I've done to your house and people flipped out over it. I have several clients lined up now. I'm back!" I said excitedly.

"I'm happy for you," he said simply. "But I'm not ecstatic about sharing you."

"It was bound to happen," I teased.

"You're right," he said seriously. "You're so talented. Gifted at your job. It's no wonder people are salivating at the mouth to get to you."

I laughed at the image his statement conjured up, but was humbled by his characterization of my work.

"Thanks for that. No one has ever called me gifted before."

"No one knows your work like I know it. At least, that's how it feels."

His compliments were beginning to make me feel a little uncomfortable. I didn't know that he thought so highly of me. I sat there in silence not knowing what else to say to him. I felt there were a lot of things left unsaid between us but I didn't know how to bring them up.

Finally, he pulled up to my apartment and we just sat there in the dark.

"Erik---" I began.

"Yes?"

I opened my mouth and closed it again, not sure how to proceed. I couldn't really see his face in the dark, and the darkness made me brave. I wanted to tell him everything. I wanted to tell him how conflicted I felt, but how I couldn't help falling for him.

But as I tried to start again, his voice cut through the darkness.

"He has a point, you know. He's kind of right. You would be a great choice for a surrogate."

"What? Are you kidding me?" I was stunned. Me? A surrogate? What was Erik talking about?

"We're friends. We're not in a relationship. No messy emotions will get in the way. It's kind of perfect."

"You're crazy."

"I don't think so. At least for once I'm thinking straight."

"What do you mean "thinking straight"? You must have bumped your head. Oliver is insane. Don't do anything he recommends."

"You're right, Oliver is a nut, but what he proposed does make sense."

"How? We're sex buddies."

"Exactly, but we're also friends. So even though there are no strings attached, we get along. We care about each other...at least I think you care about me." His voice was soft in the darkness as he reached out and touched my face.

I could finally see his eyes and met them. "Of course, I care about you. We're friends," I said without hesitation. "Friends care about each other."

"Sounds like the perfect surrogate relationship to me."

"Even if you think it's ideal, I have no intention to rent out my uterus."

"I could pay you whatever you asked."

"It's not about the money."

"Then what is it about?"

"It's about the fact that we're sex buddies, friends.

What you're proposing will change all that. And I love what we have, I don't want to see it ruined."

"How would it be ruined?"

"Come on, Erik. What you're proposing is something couples do. Normally married couples. They plan to have babies together. Couples do that. Not friends. We're not a couple. We shouldn't even be discussing this."

"Don't you see that's what makes it so perfect? We have no ties to each other. Like you said, we're not a couple. So if you wanted to just walk away, you could. Or if you want to be part of the kid's life, you could. You have all the cards in your hand. Ultimately it's your decision."

I shook my head. Was I actually considering this? "What you're talking about is crazy. Absolutely crazy."

"I don't know. I think it's pretty perfect."

I sighed. "You're serious, aren't you?"

"As serious as a heart attack."

"You're going to give me a heart attack."

He squeezed my hand and said, "Just think about it. That's all I'm asking you. Just consider it. You don't have to give me an answer today or even tomorrow, just consider it."

We sat in silence and I covered my hand with his. "My answer is going to be no, Erik. I don't want you to think otherwise."

"I understand I just brought this up out of nowhere. But just think about it before telling me no--can you just do that?"

I sighed. It wouldn't hurt to just consider his request, right? "Okay, I'll think about it."

He grabbed my face and kissed me hard on the mouth. "That's all I can ask."

I climbed out of his car and made my way upstairs. As I undressed, I thought about Erik's words. I wanted Erik to be happy. I wanted to help him, but I didn't want to donate my body to science to make that happen.

I didn't particularly like babies and everything about hospitals and the little I knew about labor freaked me out, grossed me out, or frightened me. I was okay with bigger kids. I liked kids. I just couldn't imagine physically carrying one.

I didn't even know why I was considering it. And that thought shocked me. I was seriously considering it.

So I took a chance and reached for the phone. I called Emmaline.

She answered on the first ring.

"Hi, what's up?"

I sighed. "If I tell you something can you promise to keep an open mind?"

"Umm...I'll try."

"Emmaliiiine," I whined. "Pleeeeease."

"Okay, I promise. I promise."

"So Lacey, Oliver and now Erik have gotten it in their minds that I would make a great surrogate for Erik."

"Erik, Jude and Oliver's friend? The guy you're working for? He wants you to be his surrogate?"

"Well, not at first, but Lacey and Oliver keep bringing it up."

"Lacey? That's surprising."

"I think she just wants everyone to be pregnant with her. She even planned to ask you if you and Colin were planning to have another."

Emmaline laughed dryly. "Well, that's not going to happen. Like definitely not going to happen. As in, I took steps already to ensure no more babies pop out of me. And Colin's going for the big snip too. We agreed that Theodora was going to be an only child."

I laughed.

"But back to your problem...isn't that a little awkward? Your client asking to borrow your uterus? Sounds weird."

"Well," I said hesitating, "he's not just my client. We've been, uhhh, seeing each other for most of this year."

"What! And why am I just hearing about this now?!"

"I didn't want anyone to know."

"But why not? That doesn't make any sense. We just want you to be happy with whoever you're with. You didn't need to keep it a secret. I'm surprised that you would."

I took a deep breath. "Well, when I said seeing each other...I actually just meant sex." I decided to just spit it out. "We sort of have an arrangement."

"What type of arrangement?" she asked suspiciously.

"We're friends...who have sex with each other," I said quickly. I then stuck my head in my shirt, embarrassed even though Emmaline couldn't see me.

"So you're sex buddies? Friends with benefits? I guess technically so were Colin and I before we stopped playing around and got serious. I don't understand what the big deal is. Why would you keep that a secret?"

"I don't know. I just thought you wouldn't think it was a good idea, considering I've never done anything like this before and because I was recently divorced."

"You deserve a little fun. Sex is fun. Your marriage was over. From what I can tell, Erik is a good guy. You're not going to get any condemnation from me."

And that was the root of the problem. No one else was judging me but me. Hadn't Lacey encouraged me to date Erik? Hadn't Oliver even pushed it? But what we were doing wasn't dating. We were using each other, using each other for sex. It just felt a little sordid and that was the root of the problem. I was the one who deep down had a problem with our arrangement. No matter how much I told myself I wouldn't feel guilty or bad for only being sexually involved with Erik, I actually did feel bad. I felt bad because I was selling myself short yet again. I wanted more than just sex now, but instead of standing up for what I wanted, I had done the same thing I had done with my marriage, settled for less and just went with the status quo.

I needed to start being honest with myself. I had started falling for Erik the moment I laid eyes on him. The sex had just been an extra bonus. I told Emmaline all this and she listened carefully.

"So what are you going to do?"

"About the surrogate issue?"

"No. About your feelings toward Erik?"

"Nothing. There's nothing to do. I could break it off."

"But that's not what you really want."

"No. That's not what I want."

"Just talk to him about how you feel. There's a possibility that he feels the same way."

"I doubt it. He always talks about how he doesn't do relationships."

"That's bullcrap. Just because your relationship doesn't fit under a neat label doesn't take away from the fact that you guys are a couple, whether you guys acknowledge it or not. You spend all your free time together, you share things with each other, clearly you both care about each other. You guys might not have formally declared yourselves together, but your behavior states otherwise. Is he seeing anyone else?"

I thought of Candy, but didn't really believe he was seeing her. "No, no. He's not dating or seeing anyone else."

"So whether you guys admit it or not...you're in an exclusive, undefined relationship."

Emmaline was right.

"But I still don't know what to do about the surrogate issue."

Emmaline sighed. "Hon, the surrogate issue is really a non-issue. There's no way you can be a surrogate for a man that you're clearly in love with. You can't carry the baby of the man you love, give up the baby to him and then just continue with your current arrangement where you both act like you don't care for the other. That would just be stupid."

I nodded. She was right. "I know, I know, everything you're saying makes sense. I just don't know how to tell him all of this."

"Which part?"

"All of it."

"You could just start by telling him the truth. Telling him that you love him. Telling him that you want more than just hot sex in an undefined relationship."

"But what if he doesn't want the same? What if he just wants to remain friends with benefits?"

"Then for your sake, it would be best to end it."

I knew she was right but my heart hurt just thinking about it. "I have a lot to think about," I said once I found my voice again.

"Yeah, I'm sorry for clearly not giving you the answer you wanted to hear."

"I knew you would be the voice of reason."

"I just don't want to see you get hurt."

"It seems like that's the way this will all play out."

"If he has any sense at all, he'll tell you he feels the same way and then you guys will live happily ever after."

"Life isn't a fairy tale," I said sadly.

"That doesn't mean you can't have a fairy tale ending. Tell him how you feel. He would be a fool not to love you back."

"I thought Wyatt loved me," I said softly.

"I think he did, but sometimes people fall out of love. That's no excuse for cheating. But it is grounds for leaving a relationship. And you don't know if Erik is like Wyatt. Wyatt was a prick, Erik is a man desperately trying to start a family. They shouldn't even be put in the same category."

We got off the phone shortly after that. I was in deep thought contemplating my conversation with Emmaline. She had been right about everything. There was only one thing left for me to do. I would just tell him. Tomorrow. I would tell him tomorrow how I felt.

9

———

I was a coward. I didn't tell Erik how I felt the next day. I didn't even tell him how I felt the day after that. Instead, I told myself that I would wait until the conversation occurred naturally. But now that I was fully accepting of the fact that I had let Erik into my heart, I was having a hard time not telling him.

Thankfully he didn't mention the surrogate issue again. And after a couple of weeks, it was almost as if that conversation had never happened. We were back to our normal playful selves.

In fact, I was finishing up his nursery when he came in catching me off guard.

"Hey there," I said, busily arranging the decorative toys.

He looked around and ran his hand over the crib. He looked contemplative and sad.

"No luck yet?" I asked, afraid of the answer.

"None," he said softly.

"Can't you just lawyer up and get out of the contract?"

"I could, but that would be messy. It's not their fault finding a surrogate for me has been nearly impossible."

"That's very diplomatic of you." I didn't know what else to say. I was tense, knowing what was coming up next.

He cleared his throat and leaned his lower back against the crib. He crossed his arms in front of him and said, "So have you given what we discussed any thought?"

I nodded. "I've given it a lot of thought," I said as I lowered myself to the daybed that sat across from the crib.

"And?" he said, looking at me as if trying to read my eyes. "What did you decide?"

Now's your moment, Misha. Tell him. Come on. Just spit it out. Tell him no and tell him why you said no. Tell him that you love him. Tell him that you want to be with him. Tell him.

As if knowing my answer was going to be no he turned away and started slowly picking up the baby toys that he had already collected. And that simple motion was heartbreaking. Watching him so carefully and lovingly handle toys for a child that might never exist broke my heart. If there was something I could do to stop the hurt then I would. I hated to see him hurting.

"Yes," I said in a whisper.

"What?" he said, turning back to look at me.

"I'll do it," I said, my voice a little stronger.

"Are you serious? You're actually going to do it?"

"Yes," I said softly.

"You'll be my surrogate?"

"Yes," I said, feeling my stomach drop and my heartbeat pick up. It wasn't out of excitement. It was out of fear. What the hell was I doing?

His face instantly transformed. Gone was the weary, guarded expression, in its place was pure happiness. He pulled me up from the daybed and wrapped his arms around me and gave me a long hug. He then looked up and kissed me gently, holding my face between his hands as he did so.

"Thank you so much. Thank you for doing this for me. Thank you. Thank you. Thank you."

I finally felt at peace. I didn't know what the next 9 months would hold, but if it meant Erik's happiness, I was willing to face the unknown.

"We'll set you up an appointment with the doctor. This is so great. The greatest moment of my life." He stepped back to look at my face and said, "You made this happen. Thank you."

"You're welcome, but I also have a request. A minor stipulation."

"Sure, anything."

I took a deep breath. "I hate doctors. If I could minimize my visits there..starting with conception, that would be great."

He looked at me and took a step back. "You mean you want to conceive...naturally."

"Yes, I would prefer that to some turkey baster up my nether regions." I stared at him. "Why do you look so shocked? Is my request a problem?"

He shook his head as if to clear it. "No, of course not. I'm just surprised that's all."

"We've been having sex together for months...I'm not sure why the idea of having sex with me with a purpose in mind is so off putting." I was feeling hurt by his hesitation and surprise.

"It's not that," he said, rubbing my arms. "You just caught me by surprise. I'll gladly have sex with you to make a baby. A million times."

I smiled. "I hope it doesn't take that many times, to be honest, but if it does, I'm not too morally opposed."

"That's good to know."

"Sooo..." I said stepping back out of his arms, "when should we get started?"

"As soon as possible," he said.

"I need to catch up with a new client, but I'm free tomorrow night. You want to try then?"

"Yeah, sure. Definitely. Tomorrow. My place or yours?"

"How about yours?"

"Okay, sounds like a plan. I have to be honest. I am a little worried."

I smiled wantonly. "You? Nervous about sex? Who are you and what have you done with Erik?"

"Okay. Okay. You have a point. I'll see you tomorrow." He took my hands in his and looked deeply into my eyes. "Thank you. Thank you for this."

I stared into his eyes, wondering if I was making the biggest mistake of my life. But it didn't matter now. I intended to keep my word. I was going through with it.

I WAS nervous the next day as I waited for Erik outside of his condo in the city. But part of me was also excited. I was so conflicted and I thought to myself, all of my emotions relating to Erik were conflicting and complicated. Apparently, I liked complicated. A lot.

I hadn't told Emmaline or Lacey that I had agreed to be Erik's surrogate. I didn't know how long it would take me to get pregnant, but I decided I would just tell them once that happened. I didn't want to cause them concern, especially Emmaline who knew how I really felt about Erik.

Finally, I was ready. I raised my fist to knock on the door and realized that my hands were shaking. I knocked quickly and then saw there was a doorbell and impulsively hit that too.

My level of nervousness was up there with a virgin on her wedding night. Yikes. What was taking Erik so long? I thought crossly. I raised my hand to knock again when he finally opened the door. Erik stood there looking handsome and just as unsure as I did.

"Come on in," he said softly. "Do you want a drink?"

"Sure, I'll take one."

He poured a glass of wine each for me and himself.

"What should we toast to?"

"Friendship," he offered. For some reason, I was disappointed. Friendship and a baby, apparently that's all he wanted from me. Maybe he thought that was the best I could offer.

We took a few sips of wine and then we slowly made our way to his bedroom. The lights were low and I sat down on the bed.

He came and sat down next to me. Slowly he reached for my hand. He brought it up to his mouth and kissed my palm.

Shivers of pleasure in anticipation of more to come overtook me, but something felt different. And I knew exactly what. This night wasn't business as usual. We weren't about to have sex...we were about to make love.

I let him lower me to the bed and to my surprise he didn't try to unbutton my clothes. He just placed kisses across my face, until he came to my lips. He teased my lips, giving me soft fleeting kisses until I held his head in place and took what I wanted. I also took one of his hands and brought it up to my breast. Through the fabric of my shirt, he began to rub my nipples, alternating from one breast to the other. I was growing wet and wanted him inside me desperately.

He pulled away from me then and just stared at me as he traced a finger over my lower lip. I was nervous and I could tell that he knew.

I licked my lips and his eyes followed the movement.

"Nervous?" he asked, as he slowly unbuttoned my shirt. I could only nod as his dark eyes studied mine.

He rid me of my clothes excruciatingly slowly, taking his time to caress my body, touch me softly, dare I say even lovingly?

I was writhing in pleasure and I wanted him badly. His gentle touch, his warm kisses, the feel of his member hard and ready against my thigh had me begging him for completion.

I wanted him badly. I needed him. I needed him to complete me. I hadn't expected foreplay...or gentleness...after all, this was just lust, right? Just sex for him...then why as he brought his lips back to mine was I only thinking about how much I wanted this...us...to last forever?

Against my better judgment, the words I had been holding in so long, slipped out in a whisper, "I love you."

He had been busy kissing me and I had known that just before that moment he had been ready to push inside me to take what he wanted, to feel my wetness around his shaft. But instead he stopped and I lay there with my legs spread wide trying to catch my breath. But I could see it in his eyes. He hesitated to take me because he must have heard my words. He swore to himself and bent down to pick up my shirt. "You need to leave," he said, unceremoniously dumping the shirt in my hands.

I suddenly felt hollow inside and of course we began to fight. I didn't know how things had gotten so bitter and emotional between us, but all I knew was that I couldn't do this anymore. It was time to tell him exactly how I felt.

"We can't do this anymore. I can't do this anymore," I said, feeling desperate.

"Misha---"

"What? What do you want now, Erik?" I've given you everything, everything that I have, I thought to myself.

Without hesitation, he answered, "You."

He gathered me in his arms.

I shook my head against his chest and pushed him

away, but he didn't let me go. "I can't do this, all of this, without you knowing how I feel about you. I love you, Erik. Whether you accept it or not, whether you love me back or not, I've fallen for you. And I love you. I'm not scared to say it." I took a shaky breath and realized that I was crying. "At least not anymore."

He looked down at me, studying my eyes. He didn't say a word as his mouth closed over mine. His kiss was so soft, yet so passionate at the same time. My knees felt weak, my legs were like jelly under me, his kiss so powerful that I could barely stand.

I guess he noticed because he picked me up and laid me on the area rug in front of his bedroom fireplace. He pushed the coffee table out of the way and kneeled in front of me. He buried his head between my legs and parted my thighs with his hands. He licked me and fingered me at the same time, getting my sex ready again for his entry.

I unabashedly spread my legs further apart, granting him better access. He continued to finger me, but his tongue this time began to lick circles around my clit, not actually touching it, just teasing it so it would come out of hiding. And when it finally did he licked it softly and my hips lifted as I cried out in pleasure.

"Erik!"

He slid up next to me and began to stroke my face as his other hand expertly played with my clit. He kissed me as he did it, again with the soft, gentle kisses and he never broke eye contact with me as he lay on his side facing me, bringing me pleasure I'd never experienced before.

I came then, staring into his eyes, the force of my orgasm radiating from my center, but so powerful I had to close my eyes to experience the fullness of it as my blood seemed to rush to head. My orgasm was so strong, so intense that the aftermath made my head hurt.

And it was then that he climbed on top of me.

"You sure? Are you sure you want this? Are you sure you want me?" he asked as he rubbed his cock against my wet folds...my sex was still pulsating and I wondered if I would die from all the pleasure.

"I'm sure," I said, wrapping my arms around him. I pulled his lips down to mine as he easily slid inside me. I moaned against his lips as he stayed still inside me. Even though he didn't move my sex was still tightening and pulsing around him, echoes of my previous orgasm still present. But I wanted more and so when he didn't immediately start moving, I pressed my heels into his buttocks, lifted my hips and began to maneuver his cock in and out of me.

"Keep going, it's all yours, sweetheart," he said, before kissing me again and running his hand down the side of my thighs.

I did as I was told, but I couldn't get him deep enough. "Please, Erik...please...I need more."

He began to move then and his eyes lit up in pleasure before he buried his head in my shoulder. My hips lifted with each of his thrusts and my pussy greedily locked around his shaft, gripping his cock so that he would stay in deep. I was already coming as he thrust deeper and deeper into me.

"Erik! Don't stop! Erikkkkkk!" I screamed over and over again. I began to grind my hips with his after each thrust, trying to get him deeper while luxuriating in the feel of him stretching me, filling me, loving me.

And with that thought, my body began to spasm again and Erik kissed my collarbone where his head was buried and kept thrusting into me, deeper, faster, harder. I had to brace my hands against the wall to keep from hurting my head against it, as each of his thrusts, pushed me backward. It would have hurt if I weren't so wet and ready for him.

And to my surprise I began coming again, reaching orgasm so quickly, I wasn't prepared for the burst of pleasure that seized me. And then with one last grunt, he thrust deep into me and held himself there, suspended in pleasure as he emptied his seed into me. I shook and wrapped my arm around his back, as his warmth filled me. I was still having spasms, my orgasm still causing my sex to tighten and relax around Erik's thick shaft.

We stayed in that position for a little bit. I don't even know how long. It could have been minutes or hours. I know that I fell asleep and I was awakened when I felt him lifting me up and carrying me to bed.

I slipped between the sheets and then cuddled up next to him, my head right under his chin as I lay on his chest.

"I love you, Erik," I said again sleepily. He didn't respond. There was only silence and then I felt him take my hand and give it a small squeeze. I was too exhausted to say anything further, but I wasn't too tired to feel hurt beyond measure. I had just given my mind, body and soul to a man who clearly didn't love me.

I turned away from him and let the tears fall, as I drifted off into a troubled sleep, well aware of the person who I loved, but didn't love me in return, softly snoring next to me.

The next morning, I knew before I even turned over that he was probably gone. I sat up stiffly, sore from our lovemaking that had continued throughout the night. He woke me up at least three times during the night.

Once he had taken me roughly from behind, I remember screaming as he mercilessly pounded into me, not in pain, but in pure pleasure. He had been almost animalistic in his lovemaking. And I had liked it, no, I had loved every minute of it. And then while I was sleeping on my side, he had slipped inside me again and we had lazily made love, still half asleep, moaning as we both came simultaneously.

The rest was a blur...I just remember him being inside me, filling me with his seed, kissing my face, making tender, sweet love to me sometimes while roughly taking me other times. And now I was alone.

And honestly, I wasn't surprised. After how he reacted after I said I love you twice, it was amazing that he had even let me spend the night.

I sat up and wondered if he was even still here or if he had walked out on me and was driving to get away from me at this very moment. Maybe Simon would be outside the bedroom waiting for me with a sad expression on his face, there to explain to me that Erik would no longer be needing my "services".

I chuckled at the image my mind conjured up of Simon looking highly uncomfortable, but then as I climbed into the shower, I allowed myself to let go of the charade that I was alright and I gave myself permission to just let go. My tears mixed with the water from the shower head and I let myself cry for the mistake I had clearly made. The mistake of loving yet another man who didn't love me back. I felt humiliated, stupid, and broken.

Worst of all, it was all my fault. I had no one to blame

but myself. I was so caught up in self-blame that my brain didn't process the hands pulling me back toward a hard surface until I realized that hard surface was getting harder against my behind.

My breath caught. "I thought you left."

"Why would I do that?" he breathed against my ear as he slowly brought his hands up to fondle my breasts. He played with my nipples until they were perfect pink points.

"Bend over," he commanded and I did as I was told.

He entered me slowly, stretching me with his thick cock until he was fully buried inside of me. He began to thrust into me and I could feel his balls brushing up against me with every thrust. The water was cascading down my back drenching my hair, but I didn't care. I only cared about the feel of Erik buried deep inside me.

He began to stroke my clit with every thrust he took while keeping me balanced. My knees were buckling in pleasure...I could barely keep myself up.

"You like that, don't you? Tell me you like it, Misha. Tell me you want more."

"Moooorrreee," I said, but it came out more as a moan.

He gave me what I asked for and I wiggled my hips to give him more access.

"God, you're still tight...still so wet. I'm going to come now, Misha. I'm going to fill you..."

My nipples tightened at his words and my pussy did too. In fact, my whole body tensed and he thrust a couple more times before coming again. My sex squeezed him, gripped his cock and he groaned as he spilled his warm seed into me.

He pulled out this time immediately and helped me stand up. He turned me around to face him.

"I didn't hurt you, did I?"

"When?"

"Anytime? But especially just now?" he looked concerned and searched my face.

I shook my head. "No, you didn't hurt me. I felt good...real good," I said in a whisper, looking at the shower water puddle beneath our feet before escaping down the drain. I couldn't meet his eyes right now, there was too much unspoken between us.

He began to wash me then rubbing soap between his hands and gently cleansing me. He started off with my shoulders and then my arms. He circled my breasts and, of course, I gasped and looked up at him. He kissed me softly on the mouth and kept playing with my breasts. My breathing became irregular and he stopped. "I'm supposed to be washing you, not making you come," he said, more as a reminder to himself than to me.

"Turn around," he commanded. "Please. Your perfect breasts are distracting me."

I did as I was told, and he washed my back. It felt

good; his hands were warm and confident. He touched my body as if it were his own. I don't know why I was surprised. He laid claim to my body and my heart a long time ago.

And then to my surprise, he began to wash my hair. I recognized the scent of my favorite shampoo as he emptied it into his hand and began to massage my scalp.

In my eight years with Wyatt, not once had he washed my hair. That alone should have been grounds for divorce, I thought with amusement. Erik gave my scalp a massage and I leaned my head back as he made his way through the rest of my hair.

"That feels amazing," I said as he slowly rinsed it, threading his fingers through it.

"Almost as amazing as sex?" he asked, finally returning to his humorous self.

"Almost," I said softly, smiling a little.

When he was done with my hair he went to cut off the faucet, but I wanted to return the favor. Ten minutes later, after I had pleasured his cock with my mouth to the point where we could barely stand, we made love all over again before rinsing off and finally climbing out.

He walked out first and retrieved a towel. I stepped into it and he wrapped me up, tucking me into it like a burrito.

"Thank you."

Even though we had just been intimate, I didn't

know what to do or say anymore. Emotions were now explicitly involved and that complicated things immensely. I dried my hair with the towel as I walked into Erik's bedroom. Erik was still in the bathroom as I changed into his nightshirt. I ventured into his kitchen and saw that he had made bacon and eggs.

Everything was cold of course.

He apologized for it as he joined me at the breakfast table.

"I got distracted by your body in the shower. I had just wanted to tell you that breakfast was ready, but showering with you was too tempting to pass up."

I made a noncommittal sound in reply and kept my eyes down as I ate. Now that it was morning and we were no longer going at it like horny teenagers, the enormity of my decision and the fact that our love-making hadn't been out of love, well at least on Erik's end, weighed deeply on me.

Erik reached out to take my hand and I pulled away from him.

"Do you regret what happened between us last night?"

I looked up and met his eyes. "No."

"Tell me the truth," he said, searching my eyes for what, I didn't know. "Don't lie to me, Misha. I don't deserve that."

I scoffed. "Since when do we get what we deserve,

Erik? I deserve a man who loves me as much as I love him. I deserve a man who isn't afraid to say it. Isn't that what I deserve?"

He didn't answer the question, instead he said, "Tell me if you regret what happened between us. Do you regret that we didn't use protection?"

I dropped my fork. "Wasn't that the point? Get me knocked up. Nine months later kick me to the curb. Raise your child alone. Perfect little life. No complications. No feelings. No emotions."

His eyes became angry. "Don't fault me because you let your emotions get involved. You know I didn't want this...this conflict between us. I wanted us to be friends. I warned you that emotions would make this hard and complicated."

"It's supposed to be complicated, Erik. Love isn't easy. Love is hard."

He stood up and walked away from the table, I followed closely behind him. "You can walk away from me, but I'm not done yet. I fell in love with you and I'm not afraid for you to know it anymore. I've been hiding my feelings from you for too long. I love you, Erik." My voice caught and I continued, "And you can't tell me that you don't feel the same thing for me."

He turned around and his eyes were cold. "Why? Why does everything have to be labeled? We were fine---"

"No! You were fine. I wasn't. It was tearing me up inside, not being able to tell you how I felt. Fighting to keep those feelings from surfacing. It's been horrible. I wasn't fine. We weren't fine."

"I was fine!" he yelled at me, catching me off guard. "I was happy and so were you...but it just wasn't good enough. Being there for you, caring about you, being your lover and your friend just wasn't enough for you. What's wrong with you women, constantly wanting more, more, more? It's no wonder we men die way before you. We can't keep up with all your wants!"

"My wants? You make it sound like wanting to be loved is some sort of illness, a virus that needs to be cured."

"It is!" he said with frustration in his voice. "Before you decided that you loved me, we were happy. And now look at us. We're fighting. You're angry and hurt. I'm just plain angry and we're hurting each other for a four-letter word that means nothing."

"It might not mean anything to you, but it means a lot to me."

He placed his hands on his waist and shook his head as if he couldn't believe what was going on. "I thought we had the perfect arrangement--"

"Perfect for you," I spit out.

"Now what do we do?" he said. "Is this what we're going to bring a child into? A mother who's bitter because the father doesn't love her. And a father who's bitter because he feels betrayed by the mother."

"Betrayed? What's that supposed to mean?"

"Oh please, I know it's not a coincidence that you said you loved me after you agreed to be my surrogate. I'm not stupid. If you wanted to get married again so badly you should have found some other poor sap."

"What?" I said, not understanding, "How convoluted is your thought process? That's a rhetorical question, by the way, so please try not to answer. I don't want to marry you. I don't know if I ever want to get married again. I told you I loved you because that's how I feel. I didn't have any ulterior motives."

"You didn't or you don't?"

"What kind of person do you think I am?"

He shrugged and said coldly, "To tell you the truth, I'm not too sure anymore."

Tears threatened to escape, but I held them back. "Erik, I think I should leave."

He looked at me and said nothing for a long moment.

"You see," he said. "This is what happens when emotions get involved. Things get messy."

"You wanted this as much as I did, Erik. At any time last night you could have let me leave. You didn't have to make love to me after you found out how I felt."

He laughed nervously and said dismissively, "You're one strong temptation."

I shook my head. "I'm tempting...I'll give you that...but you wanted our lovemaking to mean something more as well. Last night and this morning were different and you can't deny it. You can blame me and be angry, but you can't deny that you feel something for me too."

"Last night, my goal was to make a baby and I did my best to ensure that happened. Nothing more. Nothing less. If you think any of last night had anything to do with my feelings, then you're sorely mistaken."

"You made love to me."

"No," he said cruelly, "I fucked you for a purpose. If you can't figure out the difference then I feel sorry for you."

His words shocked me and I wordlessly stood up and walked toward the door.

He immediately looked regretful. "I'm sorry...I shouldn't have said that."

But I was done listening. "Just shut up and leave me alone."

"Misha."

"Leave me alone!"

"But what if you're pregnant?"

I nodded. Of course, that's the only thing he cared about, using me as a vessel. "Then you'll hear from me..."

"Do I have your word?"

"I'm not the one here who can't be trusted to keep their word."

He paused and said from the doorframe, "I never lied to you. I told you I didn't want a relationship. I don't do...love."

"Love isn't something you do. It's something you feel and if I have to explain that to you then you're the one I feel sorry for."

With that, I walked away and as I took the elevator down all I could think was, "Oh God, what have I done?"

10

$\mathcal{I}$ opened my eyes and stuck my hand out, trying my best to reach my phone that normally sat on the end table next to the bed. It was pitch black in my room courtesy of the blackout curtains I had recently ordered. I hadn't been sleeping well for the past couple of weeks and I had assumed the curtains would help. They hadn't. I wasn't sleeping well because I had too much on my mind. Way too much. And by too much, I meant Erik. I wondered briefly if he thought of me like I thought of him. I wouldn't be surprised if he didn't. After all, we had just been friends with benefits until I had made the mistake of agreeing to be his surrogate. I had gotten emotionally involved against my better judgment. I was miserable and heart broken. He was probably having a blast, living it up in Monte Carlo or Thailand, wherever the richest of the rich went to hang out. So far my track record for picking the right man wasn't looking so good.

I continued to fumble around for my phone when I heard a thud as it fell down to the tiled floor. Great, it was now probably under my bed. I pictured it rolling under my bed into the abyss that I never cleaned. I groaned and leaned further over and that's when I finally noticed the time on my old-fashioned alarm clock. 4:30 AM. Who could be calling me at 4:30 AM? I was finally able to reach the phone and picked it up. Of course whoever had been calling had already hung up. It took a few seconds for my eyes to adjust to the brightness of the screen as I looked for the identity of the caller.

It was a missed call from Lacey. I was instantly awake. If Lacey was calling at this hour, something had to be wrong. I immediately jumped out of bed and began to get dressed as I called her back. She didn't answer. I tried again, practically stumbling as I tried to work myself into my jeans while balancing the phone between my ear and shoulder. The second phone call went straight to voicemail.

I didn't know what to think. I told myself not to panic. It was probably nothing. I hoped it was nothing. I laid back down thinking that she had just accidentally hit her phone while sleeping when suddenly my phone rang again. This time it was Jude's number. Now I did begin to panic.

I sat up and answered at the same time, "Jude, is everything okay?"

"Lacey's in labor."

"What?! It's too soon. Is she sure?"

I heard groaning in the background. If that was Lacey, she sounded like she was in pain.

"Was that---?"

"Yeah, we're headed to the hospital now. She insisted I call you guys first. We're leaving like right now. She wants you there."

"Okay." I couldn't think of anything else to say.

"We're going to St. Anne's. Call me when you get there and I'll send my dad down to get you."

"Okay."

He hung up before I could say goodbye or anything.

I raced across the room, grabbed my shoes, and made my way to the front door and down the stairs in record time. I was already in my car when Emmaline called.

"Did you hear--"

"Yeah, I'm heading there now. Are you?"

"Colin's out of town and I don't want to leave Dora by herself," Emmaline said.

"You don't want to bring her to the hospital?"

"Nope. Labor can be...umm...intense. And I don't want to leave her in the waiting room alone."

"I'll be in the waiting room too."

There was a long pause and then she said, "Actually, Lacey wants us in the room with her. Her doula had a family emergency so it's just her and Jude. She wants some extra support. Women preferably, or I'm sure Oliver would try to pitch in."

I bit my lip. I didn't want to be there. Birth sounded too intense for my sensibilities too. But I wasn't going to disappoint a friend.

"You can drop Dora off with Grandma. I don't think she's working today."

"That's a great idea. I'll call Grandma, I'm sure she'll watch Dora for me and then I'll head to the hospital."

"Sounds like a plan," I said happily. I wasn't too sure how much help I would be to Lacey when I was scared as well.

We said our goodbyes and I quickly made my way to the hospital. It took some time to find the visitor's parking area because the hospital was being remodeled. Due to all the construction, part of the hospital looked like it was in the middle of a war zone. There was exposed rebar and concrete everywhere; luckily that part wasn't exposed to the general public. Parking took at least another ten minutes and I hoped that Lacey hadn't had her baby yet. I briefly wondered how long it took to have a baby and I realized then that for someone who had volunteered to be a surrogate, I knew nothing about anything baby-related.

As soon as I walked into the hospital, Oliver was there to greet me. He looked anxious and worried, which made me worried. Oliver never looked worried.

"What's going on? What's happening? Is Lacey okay?"

He nodded. "Yes, she's fine. It's just that she's two weeks early. That concerns me."

"Me too," I confessed, feeling a little breathless. It wasn't until then that I realized that I had been holding my breath. I felt a little shaky. I think it was from all the adrenaline pumping through my veins.

"Where is she now? Is she waiting for a room?"

Oliver laughed, showing a hint of his usual self. "She has her own wing. I made sure of it."

"God, just when I forget you're a billionaire and think you're a normal person, you make comments like that."

He smiled and escorted me to the wing where Lacey was being taken. We passed through the general maternity ward area that was open to the public and turned down another hall where two security guards stood. They let us pass upon seeing Oliver and that's when I saw her. Jude held her hand as she walked up and down the hall, holding on to the wall, as if she were trying to claw through it.

When she saw me her face lit up and then her expression was marred in pain, as she collapsed against the wall and Jude rubbed her back looking helpless.

I ran up to her and rubbed her back too, not sure what else to do. "Are you okay? Can't they give you any meds?"

"Meds! No meds! I don't want to slow down my labor."

"But you're already two weeks early, I think you're ahead of schedule as it is."

"Grrrrrrrrrrrrrrrrrrrr" was the response I got as she bent down into a deep squat and Jude rushed to hold her hands.

"Squatting makes the contractions feel better," he told me in explanation.

I looked at Lacey who was still grimacing in pain. Her teeth were clamped together and her eyes were closed. The squats didn't seem to be working.

"Breathe, hon. One, two, three. Breath. One, two, three. Breath."

She tried and then shook her head and said, "I think your rhythm is wrong. It's supposed to be one, two---"

She never got to three as she groaned in pain. When the contraction ended she began to talk again.

"Forget this. I can't do this. I'm leaving." She started wobbling with purposeful strides toward the exit; Jude walked helplessly next to her looking unsure, but not daring to stop her. And of course, I wasn't being very helpful. I just stood there and watched the whole scene play out in front of me. Oliver and I looked at each other unsure of what to do. Lacey made it as far as the elevator before having another contraction that stopped her in her tracks.

Another mom in labor was stepping out of the elevator at that very moment. She looked calm and in charge until she spotted Lacey.

"Ohhhhhhh Godddddddddd, I feel like she's going to rip out my soul," Lacey groaned, then collapsed to all fours between the elevator doors and the other mom nervously stepped over her. Jude quickly stood between the doors to make sure they didn't close on Lacey's now prone body as she rolled over on her back and spread out like a starfish, staring at the ceiling with a stubborn expression on her face.

"If this baby wants to come out then it'll have to rip through my belly like that scene from Alien. I want no part in this."

The startled woman's husband excused himself and stepped over Lacey too. He looked back at us and gave a small unsure smile.

"She'll be fine," I found myself saying, not knowing

what else to do. "And umm…good luck with the whole birthing thing!" I called after them.

I felt so stupid, but apparently my words were appreciated. "Thanks," said the woman. "This is number five," said the man, smiling broadly.

"Five," I heard Lacey say from the ground. "She did this five times? Is she insane?"

We heaved her up and I tried to find something comforting to say. I found nothing and so I said, "I think you should stay in the unit and not try to escape."

"I think that's a reasonable plan too," Jude added. I realized then that he was sweating. The hospital was freezing so apparently he was stress sweating. Poor guy. Then I looked at Lacey; of the two, I think she deserved more of my sympathy.

"No, no, no. I don't want to do this. I can't handle this…ggggrrrrrrr," she said again, leaning up against the wall as another contraction hit her.

I heard the elevator open again and hoped it was a nurse or a doctor. Someone with medical training, because I just wanted to run away screaming. This was way too much for me.

But we got something even better.

"Hey, kiddo. Are you terrorizing everyone in the maternity ward?"

"Emmaline!" I said, so happy for reinforcements. She gave me a smile and went over to Lacey.

"You can leave now. We're all leaving," Lacey said. Jude shot Emmaline a look that clearly said help me. I briefly looked around and wondered where Oliver had disappeared to.

"Come on, you. Let's go have a baby."

Lacey's eyes filled with tears. "But I'm not ready yet."

"Well, that baby's clearly not waiting."

"I know that she's ready...but I'm not. I'm just not."

Emmaline grabbed Lacey by her shoulders and looked into her eyes, "A mother is never really ready, but you got this, Lacey, and we're going to help you. Every step of the way."

Lacey instantly stopped crying. She gripped Emmaline's hand and was about to say something when another contraction rocked her body.

She squatted again, looking almost Zen now. When the contraction was over, she gave us a shaky smile and said, "You're right. I got this."

"Cool, so I'm going to go find Oliver. I'm sure you guys can handle it from here."

"Don't go too far," Lacey said, reaching for my hand and squeezing it. "I'm about to be a mom and I want you to witness it."

"I won't miss it. I promise."

"Now, let's go get that epidural. Where the heck is the anesthesiologist?" I heard Lacey saying as she headed toward the nursing station. "Take charge." Lacey was back.

Jude and Emmaline walked on either side of her. She was in good company, I thought as I turned away determined to find Oliver to pass the time. Everyone else was busy, so I figured I would just look for him downstairs.

I made my way from the maternity ward and didn't see Oliver anywhere. Where the heck was he? I didn't think he would be so squeamish, but apparently he was. I found him outside standing in front of some sort of memorial.

"Hey there, you're missing the drama upstairs. It's pretty epic."

He didn't respond and that's when I noticed his lips quivered a little.

"Oliver, are you alright?" I said, reaching for his shoulder.

He shook his head.

"What's wrong?" I asked concerned.

"I didn't know they moved the memorial here. I wasn't expecting to see it here. In fact, I'd never seen it until today. They must have moved it here because of all the remodeling."

It was then that I saw the name in front of the gigantic statue that featured a woman sitting on a bench, holding a book in her hand, legs crossed, looking peaceful. Engraved on a stone in front of the statue were the words "In loving memory of Ophelia". It was his deceased wife's memorial.

"I guess Jude knew it was here, but it caught me by surprise." He smiled and looked up at me. His eyes were damp and red. My heart hurt for him, for this man who clearly still grieved the loss of his wife.

I didn't know what to say so I stayed silent. It seemed like I was speechless a lot today. But I needn't have worried, Oliver knew exactly what to say.

"It's fitting though, isn't it? The hospital where she died would also be the hospital where our grandchild will be born."

"The circle of life," I found myself saying. I felt that sounded stupid. I couldn't believe I was quoting the Lion King. And then I remembered that it wasn't even 6 AM yet. My brain was still asleep. And apparently, kind of worthless right now.

"I'm sorry. I'm not very eloquent right now."

He shook his head. "Hon, you could be speaking Latin for all I know right now and it wouldn't even occur to me."

I placed my head on his shoulder and said, "Let's go get some coffee and then head back up to see Lacey."

"Sounds like a plan," he said, giving the statue one last long look.

"It is quite beautiful."

"Yeah. She was a beautiful person inside and out, so

it's fitting." He stopped in his tracks then and patted his pocket. "I guess we're going to just have to beg for coffee from the nurses because I don't know where my wallet is."

"You probably just left it in your car. I can run out and check for you."

"No, no, you go upstairs..."

I shook my head and said, "Between you and me, I'm sort of hoping the baby is already here before I go back up there. Labor creeps me out." Not that I would ever experience it, I thought not for the first time since my encounter with Erik. It had been two weeks since we made love. He hadn't called or tried to contact me that first week, but once he hadn't heard from me that second week, he had called, emailed, showed up at my apartment, but I had refused to see him, let alone talk to him.

He laughed. "Me too. That's why we, Ophelia and I, stopped at one," he chuckled. "I was hiding down here when I came across the memorial."

"Yeah, I volunteered to come find you because I felt I would just be in the way up there."

"I feel the same too. You would think that in the year 2017 scientists would have come up with a way to make this whole labor thing...well, just less painful and less messy for women."

"Tell me about it. My heart started to race when we

got off the elevator on that floor and I'm not even the one in labor." I couldn't believe I had ever agreed to be a surrogate.

He laughed and handed me the keys. "It's the Tesla out front."

"Of course, it is."

I glanced at the memorial as I walked past it, wondering if anyone would love me as much as Oliver clearly had loved Ophelia. And at that moment, I accidentally dropped his keys. I reached down to pick them up when I heard a horn blare and felt an impact that ripped a scream from my throat as my body went flying through the air and I landed with a thud. A sharp pain so horrendous pierced my lower body. The pain was so bad that I felt myself losing consciousness. My head, my lower body, my hand...everything hurt. I saw Oliver standing over me with other strangers, they were talking to me. Telling me that everything was okay. Telling me to hold on, but it was too late.

PART III

11

"Misha, are you awake?"

I wanted to reply but my mouth felt dry for some reason unknown to me. I opened my eyes and looked around. I was confused by the white walls around me and the beeping machines. I tried to sit up and a pair of strong hands stopped me.

"Take it easy," said Wyatt, as he pushed me gently back into the pillows.

"Wyatt? Why are you here? Did Lacey call you?"

I was itchy, thirsty and felt a little drugged. I started scratching my arms as I looked around me. I was in the hospital. Why the heck was I in the hospital?

I groaned. I hope I hadn't fainted when Lacey went into labor. And then I remembered, I hadn't made it back to Lacey's room.

"What happened to me?" I asked Wyatt, still confused by his presence but wanting answers.

"You were hit by a car."

"Hit by a car? Now that you mention it, it does feel like I've been hit by a truck."

"It was actually a sedan. A Honda I think."

"Thanks, Wyatt. Thanks for the clarification."

"Sure," he said and then frowned. "You're being sarcastic, aren't you? Well, at least that's a sign that you're on the mend."

"What exactly did they do to me?" In a panic, I wiggled my toes just to make sure that I still could and bent my knees. I let my head fall back to the pillow and gave a sigh of relief.

"You can still walk," Wyatt said. "The surgery went really well."

"Surgery, what surgery?"

"You were injured. You went flying backward and landed on a piece of rebar. It tore through your lower abs..."

I looked down under the blanket, afraid of what I might find. "They had to operate?"

Wyatt seemed to be not telling me everything. It was something about his expression, something about how he couldn't even meet my eyes that made me suspicious.

"What's up, Wyatt? Why won't you look at me? What happened? What did they do to me?"

"St. Anne's is a great hospital, Misha--"

"That's not what I asked you. What did they do to me, Wyatt?"

He swallowed hard and looked down at his toes. After a long minute, he looked back up at me. "They had to perform reconstructive surgery on your hand. It was badly injured when the car knocked you into the construction area."

I noticed my hand then, but that wasn't my concern. What was he leaving out?

"Spit it out."

"Okay…here goes." He took a deep breath and said, "They had to remove one of your ovaries…they were able to save one. But not the other…"

"So, what does that mean?"

"You might have some difficulty conceiving…maybe or maybe not…that is, if you changed your mind and actually wanted to have children."

I shook my head…I didn't know how I felt. I'd never given my ovaries much thought, but knowing that I was missing one made me feel sad and strangely incomplete. I knew it was silly, but I felt like I needed to grieve.

"How long have I been out?" I asked to distract myself.

"I don't know. I came after your surgery. I'm not sure how long you were in surgery."

I turned away from him, not wanting him to see me

cry. And I truly felt like crying. So many emotions were running through my head. I was scared that I wouldn't get full use of my hand again. I was scared that a surgeon had left a scalpel in me. I was scared that I would somehow get sepsis and then just keel over. I was a ball of fear, nerves and anxiety. I wanted my grandma. I needed my family.

"Misha?" he asked hesitantly. "You okay?"

"Can you get the doctor for me?" I asked softly.

"Yeah, sure. I'll be back." He seemed hesitant, like he didn't want to leave me, but I didn't want him around.

I needed him out of the room so that I could cry without feeling self-conscious. As soon as he was out of the door, the tears came. I don't know why I was so upset, but I was. I was glad I was alright, but I guess waking up in a hospital without knowing what was going on and having to deal with my ex-husband was the last thing I expected when I opened my eyes.

And it was then that I felt the pain. Nearly every time I took a deep breath, I felt pain. It hurt to sob and I tried to will the pain away. God, this was miserable. Now, I kind of understood what Lacey had been going through. Oh yeah, Lacey!

I looked for my phone and found it on the nightstand near me. I called Emmaline and no one answered. I called Jude, no answer. I called Oliver and finally got an answer.

"Misha?" he asked surprised. "You're already awake? I'll be up in a few minutes! My grandson was just born!"

I smiled. "It's a boy!"

"It's a boy!" I went to raise my arm to cheer and thought better of it when a searing pain went up my side.

"I'll be up to see you shortly. I'm so glad you're awake. You had me on pins and needles."

"I'm alive. Take your time. And congratulations...Grandpa."

"This is probably one of the happiest days of my life," he confessed. I could hear the smile in his voice. We said our goodbyes and I thought about his last statement. I had thought the worst day of my life had been when my parents had given me up without a fight, but once I had gotten over that, the next worse day of my life was when Emmaline told me she was thinking of dropping out of school because she was pregnant with Dora. But we had gotten through that. And the list continued with more "worst" days...from the day I lost my business and Wyatt told me that he had gotten someone else pregnant...followed by the day that Erik decided that he didn't love me. I had gotten through all those days and I would get through this one.

I was resilient. I was tough.

Wyatt soon came back with the doctor and when the doctor referred to Wyatt as my husband, I immediately corrected him calling him my ex. The doctor looked at Wyatt with annoyance and explained to him the consequences of lying to gain entrance to a patient's room and information. Wyatt tried to look unconcerned, but I could tell the doctor's words had given him pause.

The doctor was great in other ways as well. He had an excellent bedside manner. He explained all that had happened to me and everything that they had done to help me. He even apologized because they hadn't been able to save my ovary. I had smiled up at him and thanked him for at least leaving me with one. He talked about my chances of conceiving if I ever wanted to venture down that path, which I was now conflicted over, and it wasn't as grim as I thought it would be. Apparently, lots of women conceived with just one ovary. I thought that was pretty cool. And I questioned why I was so concerned about that. I didn't want kids, right? And after I left the hospital, I swore to myself that I would just focus on me and not get involved with another man for a while, if ever again. Yes, I would just focus on me and what made me happy.

And I think that's what Uncle Niko had been trying to tell me before. He hadn't been trying to tell me not to focus on a career, he was just telling me to focus on me and my wants and needs because clearly, I had an issue trying to make others happy. My divorce hadn't even been finalized for a month when I had started my fling with Erik, a fling that had turned into much more, at least for me. And where had that gotten me? Heartbroken. I needed to try to be alone for a while. I needed to know that I would be okay just being me.

I thanked the doctor for his help and settled back against the pillow.

"Comfortable?" Wyatt asked.

"Good enough."

"I can go out and buy another."

"Wyatt, why are you even here? Who called you?"

"Your grandma---"

"Grandma?!" She had never been a fan of Wyatt. I'm not sure why she called him.

"Yeah, she called and started yelling at me about you not having health insurance and how the least I could do was pay for your hospital bill."

I had to laugh, that sounded like my grandma.

He laughed too. "It took me a while to figure out what she was talking about and what was going on. Your family has always been a bit eccentric."

I shrugged. "Crazy. Go ahead. You can say crazy."

"And I did take care of the hospital bill. I told them to send it to me and paid an advance up front."

"I know you expect me to thank you, but you lied about our relationship to get that bill in your name."

"I did what I had to do. I felt I owed you at least that much."

"Well, thanks for that...because Grandma's right, I don't have insurance..."

"It's no problem..." He moved closer to me and said, "For what it's worth, I still care about you, Misha. I know I screwed up, but if you're ever interested in giving me a second chance, I would take it in a heartbeat."

I stared at him. Looking in his eyes, all I saw was sincerity. There was no guile, no ulterior motives. He was speaking the truth...at least his version of it.

I met his eyes and said, "Remember how you said we should have ended things between us a long time ago?"

He nodded. "But I didn't mean that...we had our problems...all couples do..."

"Yeah, but you were right. We should have ended things between us a long time ago. We wanted different things from each other, different things from our marriage. Our marriage dissolved for a reason. We weren't compatible from the beginning. It was just a classic form of opposites attract."

"Don't dismiss our whole marriage...We had some pretty good times."

"When we were actively engaged in each other's lives, yes. Otherwise we were just roommates who had sex with each other."

"We loved each other, Misha."

"At the very beginning, I think we did, but the rest of our marriage was just us playing our respective roles."

He sighed, placed his hands on his hips and studied the ground before looking back at me. "You're right."

I smiled sadly. "I know I am." I reached out my good hand to him and he took it. "Thanks for being here for me, Wyatt, but that's not your role anymore."

He looked at me for a long time and then leaned down and kissed my forehead. "You deserved better than how I treated you."

"Yes, and we both deserved better than each other. Except you cheated...so maybe you're a little less deserving...actually a lot less deserving."

"Yeah, I'm in therapy for that now."

"How's it working out?"

He blushed and ran a hand through his hair. "So far so good..."

I stared at him and said deadpan, "You're sleeping with your therapist, aren't you?"

He gave me a boyish shrug. "We just clicked."

I rolled my eyes. "Get out, Wyatt."

"Funny," came a voice from the door, "I was just about to say the same."

"Who are you?" Wyatt said, turning in Erik's direction. The two of them being in the same room did some weird stuff to my tummy or maybe that was the anesthesia wearing off.

"Erik meet Wyatt, my ex-husband. And Wyatt meet Erik, my, uhhh, ex-client."

"Client?" Wyatt said with a question in his voice. He narrowed his eyes at Erik and Erik glared back; he walked slowly toward Wyatt who instantly stepped back. I thought Erik was going to hit him and then he circumvented him and came over to stand beside me.

He held a huge bouquet of multi-colored roses. "I didn't know what color you liked, so I got them all."

I reached for them and then caught myself. He was the last person I wanted to take gifts from. Instead, I said dismissively, "I'm not a fan of flowers."

"Misha, I'm going to leave now," Wyatt said, giving Erik a suspicious glance.

"Okay. Thanks again, for helping," I said, wondering if I were a bad person for taking my ex's money. He had plenty of it though and it wasn't as if I had asked for it. My grandma had though. You had to love her. That woman was full of surprises.

Wyatt tried to kiss me on my forehead again and Erik caught him by the shoulder at the same time I was turning my head away from the kiss.

"Hey! Get your hands off me!"

And to my surprise, Erik unceremoniously pushed Wyatt through the door.

"I can't believe you were married to someone like that," Erik said as Wyatt huffily walked away.

"Well, I dated someone like you...and that didn't turn out much better."

Clearly, he wasn't there to argue with me as he didn't respond at all to my caustic comment. He just let his eyes run over me.

"I hate seeing you here...like this..." he finally said. "Are you in pain?"

"A little."

"Are you taking something for it?"

"Yeah, all the good stuff. At least, I think it's the good stuff."

He chuckled and said, "You sound sort of giddy."

"Well, let's see, I came here to support my pregnant best friend and instead ended up getting plowed into by someone who didn't even have the common decency to stop."

"It was a hit and run?" Erik asked angrily.

"That's what the doc said. So I'm more than sort of giddy. I'm scared, upset, scared again."

"You have every right to be scared," he reached for my good hand and I used it to toss a pillow at him instead.

He easily caught it. "I don't need you to tell me that I have a right to my own emotions, Erik."

He was annoying me and his presence was unnerving. "Who told you I was here?"

I didn't want to continue talking about my emotions. And I hoped the change of subject wasn't too noticeable.

"I called to check on Lacey and Oliver told me what had happened. He was really upset and I could barely understand him."

"Yeah, it was crazy. I just bent down to pick up his keys and the car came from nowhere."

He nodded. "I'm glad you're okay. I feel like I lost years of my life when Oliver told me what happened."

I shook my head. "This all feels so surreal. Anyway, what are you doing here? I thought you went out of town." Oliver had mentioned something like that, but I hadn't asked for any details. Besides Emmaline, no one knew of my disastrous arrangement with Erik.

"I came back when I heard."

"Sorry."

"There's nothing to be sorry for. You're more important than a business trip, especially that one. They didn't even plan to play golf."

"What's a business trip without golf? Cheapskates."

"Tell me about it. Anyway, I'm here to take you home after you get discharged."

"That's nice of you, but I plan to make other arrangements."

"Come on, Misha. Let me help you."

"I don't think that's a good idea, Erik."

He shook his head. "I told Oliver that I would take

care of you, so let me do that. Besides, I spoke to your grandma. She insisted that I pick you up. Apparently, she's heard of me before and is a huge fan."

I never yelled at my grandma but I wanted to this time.

"Okay, after I'm discharged you can drop me off at my house, but that's it."

"That's all I'm asking for. I just want to be sure you get home safely." With a final long gaze, he started digging in his pocket for his keys. I could tell he was just fidgeting, trying to ignore the awkwardness that I also felt between us.

Finally, he gave in, reached for my hand and I forced myself to pull my hand away. He looked hurt by the motion, but didn't comment on it. Instead, he said again, "I'm so glad you're okay."

"I'm glad to be alive too. I wouldn't want it any other way, but let's keep things platonic. No more touching or anything, okay?"

"I just touched your hand. That's about as innocent as it gets."

"Innocent touch or not, I would prefer not to go down that road again."

He looked like he wanted to argue with me, but then changed his mind. "You're the boss."

"Yes, I am," I said, meaning it.

He waited with me silently as the nurse described the

discharge procedures and a patient care assistant came to put me in a wheelchair.

"I don't need a wheelchair," I whined as she forced me to sit in it.

"Sorry, ma'am, hospital policies."

For some reason, the idea of riding in a wheelchair when I could walk totally bothered me.

"The quicker you get in that wheelchair, the quicker we can get you home," Erik offered, much to my annoyance.

I knew Erik had a point, but I wasn't going to give Erik credit for anything.

Minutes later, I was sitting in Erik's sports car. The patient care assistant kept telling us that we made such a cute couple. I didn't bother to correct her after the first time. I was exhausted.

"I'm sorry I didn't think to bring a better passenger car."

"I'm sorry too. This car is stupid."

"It's better than my motorcycle."

"The motorcycle has its merits. Hey, do you think you could pull this fancy shmancy car of yours into the parking garage?"

He looked at me strangely. "Why?"

"I want to sneak upstairs and see Lacey's baby."

"Lacey had her baby already?! But I thought she was

in false labor or something. Wasn't she due in like two weeks?"

"Apparently her baby had other plans."

"So, let me get this right, you want me to sneak you back into the hospital, even though you just had surgery and you were just discharged?"

"I'll only stay for a minute."

"A minute?"

"Yeah. I promise."

He looked at me and then sighed. "I shouldn't be doing this."

"It's the least you can do for me," I said testily.

He sighed again. "Okay, let me call Oliver."

Oliver appeared minutes later and between the two of them they helped me out of the car. As I approached the private door that led to Oliver's wing of the hospital, I noticed a wheelchair there.

"Seriously, Oliver? Please tell me that's not for me."

"Okay. It's not for you."

I smiled gratefully and then squeaked in rage when they proceeded to try to lower me into it. I couldn't exactly fight back without hurting myself, so instead I just stewed silently after I threatened both of them.

"Lying is bad. Just in case neither of you were aware of that."

"Duly noted," said Oliver dryly. He smiled broadly at

me and then glanced back at Erik who was pushing my wheelchair.

I folded my arms across my chest as best as I could with a busted-up hand and within a few minutes we were entering a section of the hospital that I hadn't seen before. It looked more like a hotel than a hospital.

"So, this is where they keep all the VIPs," I said in awe.

Oliver laughed. "Only the best for my family."

I spotted Emmaline and Jude first, outside in the hall chatting with each other. Emmaline squeaked when she saw me and hurriedly made her way to my side, hugging me gently.

"Oh my God...I'm so happy you're alright. I was so scared." And then she started crying. To my chagrin, I started crying too. I wasn't sobbing, but tears were certainly streaming.

I finally pulled away and awkwardly pat her on the back. "I'm okay. Everything's fine. I can even walk, but they made me sit in this thing."

She laughed. "You're the one who just had surgery and yet you're trying to comfort me."

"The irony of it all..." Oliver commented, making us laugh.

Jude had made his way over as well. "I'm sorry my dad almost got you killed, but I'm glad you made it out of surgery in one piece."

"Good job making an old man feel guilty," said Oliver heatedly. I knew the two of them were going to get into a fight right then and there, so I tried my best to head them off.

"Well, technically I'm not in one piece...I'm technically missing a piece."

"Oh, I'm sorry, Misha. I didn't know. I apologize for being insensitive--"

"See how your tasteless joke hurt her feelings," Oliver spit out.

"See how forgetting your wallet can get someone killed."

"Guys...guys...can I see Lacey and the baby?"

They immediately stopped going at each other's throats and smiled. "Baby Sebastian is beautiful," Oliver said tearing up. "He looks just like me."

Jude laughed, "No, he doesn't."

Oliver ignored him and said to me instead, "You've seen me cry a lot today. I hope you don't think I'm losing my mind."

"Not your mind, just the wall you built around your old, grubby heart," Jude said matter-of-factly.

"Thanks, Son."

"You're welcome, Dad."

And with that, Jude tossed his arm around Oliver's shoulder and we followed them into Lacey's room.

She was just waking up it seemed and baby Sebastian

was just starting to wake up too. She spotted me and gave me a big smile before reaching for the baby as she admonished me.

"What are you doing up here? You're supposed to be healing from surgery."

"It was pretty minor surgery. The impact of the car hitting me just pushed me into a pile of rebar."

She winced. "That sounds excruciating."

"So does labor."

She rolled her eyes, "Twenty-four hours...I was in labor for 24 freaking hours! At the end, I wanted them to just kill me...but I birthed this beautiful bundle of joy."

I looked at baby Sebastian who looked straight at me and made cute baby cooing noises. He was a beautiful baby, with just a tiny curl of hair, a single strand on his little bald head. He reminded me of Oliver. I said so and the rest of the room laughed.

"Want to hold him?"

I shook my head no, but Lacey was already putting him in my arms. I guess she didn't notice that I didn't have full use of both hands.

I awkwardly held him with my forearms in my lap since I was still seated in the wheelchair and to my surprise, it was Erik who helped adjust him in my arms.

"Don't be nervous," he said

"How can I not be nervous? He's tiny!" I said in a loud whisper.

"You're doing great." He then said, "Mind if I hold him?"

Lacey nodded and Erik gently removed baby Sebastian from my arms. I was relieved. Erik held him in his arms and started to talk to him. Sebastian snuggled up close to Erik and I watched them.

My heart went out to Erik. He clearly wanted more than anything to be a father. Well, I was out of the running to make him one, I thought to myself as he handed the baby to Jude.

"We should get going. I promised you a minute and you already had about ten."

I nodded knowing he was right. And I felt just really tired. I squeezed Lacey's hand and told her congratulations. I gave Jude and Oliver a hug and let Erik and Emmaline push me back into the wheelchair.

"Can't I just walk like a normal person?"

"Just in case you haven't noticed, you can't quite walk like a normal person yet." He was right. I was barely shuffling along.

"Come on, stop being stubborn. Sit down," Emmaline said.

I did as she said and waved at her until she disappeared from view. On the way back to Erik's car, I didn't have much to say, but the silence between us was deafening.

When he finally helped me into the car and then

came around to the driver's side, I tried my best not to look at him. Maybe it was all the medications running through my system, but I was starting to feel a little melancholic again.

"Sooo...you seemed really comfortable with the baby."

He shrugged. "I used to volunteer in a neo-natal unit."

"Really?"

"Yeah, that's how I met Candy."

"The skank doctor?"

He laughed. "Yes, the skank doctor. She was working at one of the hospitals where I was volunteering and we became friends."

I scoffed. "You can stop with the act. We all know you're not a boy scout."

"And I've never claimed to be," he said cutting me off. "But Candy and I have always been just friends."

"Did she get that memo?"

"She wanted more, but I wasn't interested." He stopped at a red light and looked down at me. I immediately turned my face away, I felt too vulnerable to meet his eyes head on.

"Believe it or not, you were the only woman I was sleeping with. Even though our relationship, if you want to call it that, was unconventional, I wasn't involved with anyone else while we were together."

I kept my face turned away. I didn't know what to say. And frankly, I didn't really believe him.

"So why were you hanging out with Candy if you guys were just good friends?"

"She mentioned the surrogacy program to me. She also was the person introducing me to pediatricians, like I mentioned. She was actually really helpful until she found out I was dating you and had a fit."

"We weren't dating...we were just---"

"Just, what? What would you call it?"

"Fooling around. You know sex buddies."

"Well, however you want to define our undefinable relationship is fine. But Candy got angry and removed herself from my life."

"I can't pretend that I'm upset about that."

"Me neither."

That comment caught me off guard and I found myself chuckling. I gave a big yawn immediately after and said to Erik, "Wake me up when we get there, alright?"

"Sure thing. Get some sleep. I'll wake you up later."

I closed my eyes and then slowly opened them again. "Thanks, Erik," I said softly before closing my eyes and drifting off into a long, much-needed sleep.

12

"Wake up, sleeping beauty," Erik said.

I struggled to open my eyes. I was so tired. So tired.

"Thanks for dropping me off," I mumbled as I maneuvered out of the car. Erik extended his hand to me and I took it. I was too tired to tell him off.

I tried to wake myself up and I looked around. I realized that I didn't know where we were.

"Where are we?"

"My other condo in the city. It was close to the hospital."

"I'm not staying in your condo. Take me home."

"You don't have anyone at home who can take care of you."

"So what? I can take care of myself."

"Come on, Misha. Let's not fight."

"We're not fighting," I said matter-of-factly. "I'm just telling you what you need to do and what you need to do is take me home."

"You heard the doctor. You should have someone with you just for a little while. And you're all alone in your apartment. "

I narrowed my eyes at him. "And what's wrong with being alone?"

"Everything!"

"What?!"

"I mean, nothing, but in this case, you shouldn't be alone and I wouldn't feel right just leaving you."

"Really? You didn't have a problem doing it before."

He had to visibly retain control of his anger at my comment. "I'm not trying to fight with you. I just want to make sure you're not alone so soon after leaving the hospital...anything can happen."

I stared at him and said, "I'm not pregnant."

"What?" he said, clearly confused.

"If that's why you feel some sort of misguided obligation toward me then you might as well know the truth now. I'm not pregnant."

He swallowed hard. "The accident--you didn't--did it--"

I shook my head. "I didn't miscarry either. My period actually came on the week after our little evening of ill-repute."

He looked relieved and for some reason that hurt me to the core.

"Did you hate the idea of being tied to me so much that you're thankful I'm not pregnant?"

He reached out to touch me and I hit at his hand. "It's not like that at all--"

"I'm not naive---"

"I didn't say you were---"

"I know a look of relief when I see it!" To my surprise, I was crying now.

He tried to touch me again and I fought against him as he tried to bring me into his arms. "Stop fighting me. Stop fighting me. You're going to hurt yourself. Just let me hold you. Let me hold you."

The tears wouldn't stop flowing now. I tried to pull away from him again and hurt my hand in the process. I cried out and he gently cupped it.

"See what you made me do?" I said between sobs.

"I'm sorry," he whispered. "For everything. I'm sorry."

"That's a lot to be sorry for," I managed to say between breaths.

"I did this to us and I'm sorry. I was wrong to ask you to be my surrogate. I ruined things between us. And I just want a chance---"

"A second chance to hurt me?"

"A second chance to be your friend again," he

squeezed my functional hand. "I miss you. I miss you so much."

I miss you was a far second place from I love you, but it was a start.

"Maybe just a little part of you misses me too?"

I shrugged. "Maybe a very microscopic piece of me misses you too, but I'm not staying here...I can't."

"Just for the night...come on..." He extended his hand and I stared at it. Take it, Misha, I said to myself. It's not where you want to be, but at least it's a step in the right direction.

And so I took his hand and he pulled me close, about to kiss me...I almost let him, when I caught myself and placed a finger against his warm lips.

"Just friends...that's all Erik..."

He looked like he wanted to argue, but something in my eyes stopped him.

"I understand," he straightened and slowly pulled away from me. "It's your call and I respect that."

"Thanks. Now, I'm tired...lead the way."

He didn't let go of my hand and I prayed that I could handle just being friends. Could you really be just friends with the man you loved...even if he didn't love you back? Unfortunately, I was going to find out.

* * *

"HOW ARE YOU DOING?" Grandma asked as she pushed the grocery cart through the store for me. I was going to physical therapy for my hand and had had several follow-up procedures done as well.

"Fine. Just fine."

"How's physical therapy going?"

I groaned. "My physical therapist is a pushy, bossy, results-driven maniac," I sighed. "He's great."

Grandma laughed. "Glad to hear it."

"You know, Grandma, you don't have to come with me everywhere."

"Well, with that bad hand of yours, you need someone around to help out."

"My hand is getting better."

"Not better enough. How's your friend doing?"

"Friend?" I asked as we went down the cereal aisle. I felt old. There were so many brands that I didn't recognize. What happened to plain old Captain Crunch or Fruit Loops? I thought to myself.

"That friend of yours, your man friend."

"You mean Erik?"

"Yeah. I adore him. You should too. He's so helpful and sweet. Way better than that Wyatt."

"Granny, we've been through this...Erik is just my client."

"You have the hots for him. I can tell."

I stopped in my tracks and blushed. I suddenly felt

like a teenager again. "Grandma!" I hissed, embarrassed. "Don't say things like that!"

"Well, he has the hots for you too. He rescued you like you were Sleeping Beauty."

"He brought me home from the hospital," I said dryly. "That's not rescuing. That's just transporting."

"And he made sure you were okay. He stayed by your side the whole night. Instead of running off and having sex with his secretary."

"Wyatt didn't run off with his secretary...Wait, why am I defending Wyatt?" I said out loud.

She shrugged. "A brief moment of insanity, I'm sure."

"Speaking of insanity, when did you turn into such a romantic?"

She smiled. "I've always been a romantic. In fact, I have a date tomorrow."

"With whom?" I was instantly curious and reached out to stop the grocery cart. "Come on, tell all. You can't just drop news like that on me and then continue to shop like it's no big deal. You haven't had a date in what? 20? 30 years?"

She shot me a cold look. "Five. Five days."

I stared at her. "Who are you and where have you taken my grandma?"

"Well, there are lots of bachelors in the old folks' homes. Lots of hot men just waiting to set their eyes on a woman like me. You know the young didn't invent sex. It's not just for the youth!"

I covered my ears. "Stop. Stop. Stop. Lalalalalalalalalala," I started to say over and over.

She placed a hand on her hip. "Just when I thought you were a mature adult, this happens."

I uncovered my ears and said, "Okay, so where'd you meet your date?"

"Which one? The one I'm seeing tomorrow?"

My mind was officially blown. "Oh, jeez, Grandma, how many guys are you seeing?"

"Two or three...one just wants to be friends, but I know he's just playing hard to get."

I shook my head. My love life was nonexistent while Grandma's love life apparently never had a dull moment.

"Anyway, the guy I'm seeing tomorrow was a guy I met at work."

"You're dating a coworker?"

"Well, technically he's a client."

"Client?" I laughed, "Granny, you're a telemarketer. How did you meet your client? Hold on, Granny, did you pick someone up over the phone? Is that how you met him?"

She smiled. "We talked for hours. I totally forgot I was supposed to be selling him timeshares in Miami."

I laughed. I couldn't believe it.

"When I found out he was local, well, I just got so excited and we agreed to meet up."

"That's wonderful. Well, be sure to meet, you know, in a public place. You might think you know him, but he's still a stranger."

My grandma scoffed, "Hon, this isn't my first rodeo. I used to date guys off craigslist all the time."

"You did not!"

"I did too."

I shook my head. "How did I never know this?"

She shrugged. "You never were around and you never really asked."

I instantly felt bad. "Was I really that self-absorbed these past years?"

"No. You were just busy living your life. No one can fault you for doing that. Speaking of which, maybe you should give that Erik fella another shot."

"Or not," I mumbled. My grandmother didn't know the whole story. She only knew that he wasn't interested in a relationship.

And of course, my mind immediately turned to Erik. He had been taking me to my appointments and helping me out with various tasks that related to my interior design business. He had been pretty great, just very helpful and caring. He anticipated my needs and always made sure to be available. I knew he had canceled meetings and delegated his usual duties to others to help me out and I truly appreciated it. He had even sent Simon to run errands for me when he couldn't miss a meeting. He was a true friend. It was too bad my heart yearned for a lot more than a platonic friendship.

But a platonic friendship was what I was going to get. In fact, I was seeing Erik later that evening. He was coming over to see me and bringing dinner so that we could wrap up a few details about his home, nothing more, but I didn't want to tell Granny that. She would pry and ask questions that I really didn't know the answer to. It was hard enough trying to figure out how to deal with my emotions without having to explain to someone else how exactly I felt.

LATER THAT NIGHT, as I waited for him at my home, I couldn't help but second guess myself. Maybe I should have agreed to meet him at a bar instead or just anywhere else but my apartment. I didn't feel comfortable being alone with him because it was getting harder and harder to ignore my feelings for him. I thought over time my feelings wouldn't be as strong, but I was wrong. If anything, the time we spent together, just as friends, made me love him more.

I looked in the mirror a few minutes before he was

scheduled to arrive. I had on a graphic tee and a pull-on mini-skirt. Zippers were still hard for me to handle.

A minute later, Erik showed up and to my surprise, he was empty-handed. Well almost, he held his helmet in one hand.

I looked at him and frowned. "Where's the food? Remember you agreed to bring dinner?"

"Yeah about that. I thought we could go out. You know, to celebrate a job well done."

I looked down at what I was wearing. "I'm not exactly dressed for a night out."

"What are you talking about?" he said giving me an appraising look. "You look fine."

He then surprised me by handing me a helmet as well. He had been hiding it behind his back.

I took it without thinking. "What am I supposed to do with this?"

"We're going on a ride."

"I don't want to go on a ride. I want to sit on my couch, watch SpongeBob and eat Chinese."

"All those things sound great, but I have something better planned."

"I don't know..."

"Come on...trust me."

I sighed and he gave me a big smile, knowing that I had already given in.

"You're going to love this." He grabbed my hand and dragged me toward the door.

His enthusiasm was infectious and I found myself wondering what he had in store for us. His motorcycle that I hadn't seen since we first met sat in front of my apartment.

"I'm wearing a mini-skirt. How am I expected to ride this and maintain a semblance of decency?"

He laughed as he put on his helmet. "You aren't." He shoved my helmet on and then climbed on. "Come on, your chariot awaits." I hesitated and then said, "What the hell...I might as well."

I hiked up my skirt a little more and joined him. My breasts were pressed against his back and I was able to lace my arms around his middle.

He touched my weak hand and said, "You're okay?"

I nodded. "Just start off slow---"

"Yes, ma'am," he said as the motorcycle roared to life. I gripped him as tightly as possible.

He slowly made his way through the neighborhood. "This is great."

"Huh?"

"This is great!" I yelled.

"Glad you're having fun!"

I pumped a fist in the air and giggled.

I started getting used to the ride and leaned into corners as he did. I especially appreciated that I could hold him and touch him without repercussions. He felt good...and I had to resist running my hands up his abs.

I breathed in deeply, inhaling the scent of him. I used that moment to relax against him. I knew I was enjoying the ride so much because it gave me an excuse to hold and touch him.

"Don't get too comfy," he said as we stopped at a light. "We're almost there."

The light turned green and he accelerated and I giggled. "I love this!"

I heard him chuckle in response.

We were eventually on open road and I yelled, "Go faster!"

He apparently heard me and accelerated easily as we passed through a marshy area, not too far from the beach. The landscape started to change as the city disappeared and sandy beaches and mangroves dotted the surrounding area.

He slowed down and I marveled at the view of the beach at sunset. And I knew I would remember this moment forever.

We pulled up to the beach and I was sad the ride was coming to an end.

"Isn't the beach closed at sunset?" I asked as he helped me off his bike.

"For some people..."

"I forgot...another billionaire perk?"

"Being loaded has its advantages."

I laughed. "You sound like Oliver."

"Ouch, don't insult me like that." The smile on his face belied his words. He took off my helmet and his own.

He laughed as he looked at me and I self-consciously attempted to fix my hair. "What?"

"You have helmet hair."

"Well, help me fix it. You have a mirror?"

"Leave it be. It's cute."

He led me across the beach and I could see in the distance a white tent had been erected on the sand.

"I take it that's where we're headed."

"You guessed right."

I then saw Simon standing there beaming at us. He was wearing a white suit and I had to admit he looked really sharp.

"Hey, Misha," he said. "What do you think of the suit?"

"I think I saw Snoop Dog wear something similar to an MTV awards show," I assured him.

His eyes lit up. "Seriously?" He then looked at Erik. "See, Big E, I told you. I told you this suit was sweet. You just don't understand urban sophistication."

"Why are you wearing urban sophistication on a beach?"

Simon shook his head as if he felt sorry for Erik.

"Misha, explain to him about style because clearly I'm not getting through to him."

"I'll do my best, Simon, but you know Big E, when he has his mind set on something, it doesn't change easily."

Erik frowned. "I don't know about that. I think I'm pretty open minded."

Simon looked at me and I Iooked at him and we both snickered.

"What?" Erik said, looking from me to Simon. "What was that look all about?"

"Nothing," Simon said with a smile in his voice. "Just text me when you're done and I'll come clear everything out."

"Thanks, Simon," I said as he left. Erik echoed my thanks.

"Not a problem. You guys enjoy." Simon then winked at me as Erik turned away and I stuck my tongue out at him. I heard him laughing softly to himself as he walked away.

"So, what's the plan, Big E?"

He looked pained. "Please don't call me that. Simon started calling me that last year and it drives me nuts."

"Did you tell him to stop?"

"I even tried to pay him to stop. The kid's incorrigible."

"I could see how that's true...it's like you hired a little you."

He looked back at me. "Am I really that bad?"

"Well, Simon does have a better sense of fashion, but you're both pretty head-strong and do what you want."

"I never thought of myself that way."

"Well, that's the benefit of standing on the outside and looking in. You can see things from all perspectives. I imagine you and Oliver were a lot like how you and Simon are now."

He sat down and thought about it. "Now that you mention it, I guess we were. I called Oliver Rich Dude for the longest time, just to mess with him."

"When did you stop calling him that?"

"When I made my first million and he turned the tables and started calling me Rich Kid."

I had to laugh. That sounded like Oliver.

"So, what do we have here?" I asked as I looked around at the spread in front of us. There were several tables with food prepared. Lots of seafood, fruit and breads.

And a chocolate fountain? "Is that seriously a chocolate fountain?"

"Simon insisted on ordering it. I thought it was cheesy."

"It is...in a funny way." I picked up a marshmallow and stuck it on one of the long toothpicks sitting next to the fountain. I covered the marshmallow with chocolate and promptly stuck the whole thing in my mouth.

"If I had known you would go straight for the sweets, I wouldn't have ordered all this food."

"Don't worry. I'll eat that too; I'm famished."

And true to my word, ten minutes later, I had eaten two bowls of shrimp and five more chocolate-covered marshmallows.

I looked out from under the tent. The sun was sitting low on the horizon, turning the sky brilliant shades of purple and orange.

I could see an island of mangroves out on the water and I was pretty sure the faint skyline all the way across the water, in the far-off distance, was the city. Civilization seemed so far away and for a moment it felt like the world was only occupied by the two of us.

He sat down on the sand and motioned for me to join him. I lowered myself gingerly next to him, pulling my skirt down a little, as it kept trying to run up my thighs.

"I just want to say thank you for all you've done. The house, everything is spectacular. You far exceeded my expectations. You really turned my house into a home."

"I'm glad you feel that way. Thanks for choosing me. It was probably my most challenging project, a true learning experience. So, thank you for that."

He turned and studied me, not saying a word.

"What?" I said, growing uncomfortable under his gaze and hesitant to meet it.

"Nothing. I just miss looking at you."

I shifted on the sand, trying to get comfortable, but also trying to avoid his eyes. Our friendship was fragile at best and I didn't want my messy emotions ruining the night.

"You see me all the time."

"But not nearly enough."

"Well, we both have our own lives...sooo…" I let my voice trail off.

We settled into silence and finally I couldn't take it anymore. The elephant in the room, or rather on the beach, needed to be addressed.

"I think it would be best if after tonight we stopped seeing each other."

He turned to me, clearly stunned. I didn't meet his eyes, I just continued looking over the peaceful waves that were now lapping at the shore. The setting was perfect for romance, but romance was the last thing on my mind.

"What are you talking about?"

"You know what I'm talking about."

"I don't. Please clarify."

"I can't just be your friend, Erik. It hurts too much," I said, my voice breaking a little. I cleared my throat and tried again. "I just can't do this. It hurts being with you, but not being "with" you." When he continued being silent, I found myself becoming annoyed. "And what is all this anyway?" I gestured to the tent and the beach. "Why couldn't you just be like a normal person and buy me a bottle of wine as a thank you or a gift card?"

"I wasn't trying to upset you. I thought it was a nice gesture, that's all."

"Really? A romantic dinner on the beach was your idea of a nice gesture?"

"I'm not sure why you're angry with me about trying to do something nice for you." His voice was calm but angry. He didn't have a right to be angry as far as I was concerned. He wasn't the hurt party here.

"I'm just tired of getting mixed signals from you. You treat me like a girlfriend, tell me you only want me to be your lover. Then you invited me to be your surrogate and then realized that you only have friendship to offer?"

"Look, I ---"

"I'm not done yet. It's no wonder that I've been feeling confused and conflicted throughout our relationship. Oh, I'm sorry...that's right--we're not in a relationship."

"I'm not sure why we have to rehash--"

"Because it's not fair! This is not fair to me. You can't have your cake and eat it too. You can't decide that one day you want to treat me like your girlfriend and the next just your friend with benefits, and then the next day just your bestie. Do you know how screwed up that is? Do you know how much you hurt me?"

"That's not what I was trying to do. Like I said, I just wanted to say thank you---" He turned and looked at everything. "But I can see how you might get confused--"

I stood up then. "I'm not the confused one. You are. I know what I want. But apparently, you're still trying to figure it all out."

"I told you already...I was just trying to be nice."

"By creating a romantic getaway on the beach, by getting my adrenaline going by taking me on a motor-cycle ride where I spent at least 30 minutes pressed up against you? You need to make up your mind, Erik."

He shook his head and stood up. "You already know how I feel..."

"Really? Care to tell me?"

"We're friends...I thought once you got out of the hospital, we had agreed---"

"Friends don't take each other on romantic private getaways."

"Okay, maybe I do...maybe I do want to be more than friends," he finally confessed. "I do want things to go back to the way they were before. But what's so bad about that?"

"When we were screwing around with each other

with no strings attached? That's what you want to see happen again?"

"You make it sound dirty...you know it was more than that."

"Was there really more than that? Honestly, was there, Erik?"

He looked frustrated as he said, "I cared for you then...I still do now." He reached up to touch my face and I pulled away. He sighed. "Just because I refuse to give our relationship a label doesn't mean it isn't important to me. You're important to me."

"I'm important to you? You care about me? And yet you can't tell me that you love me?"

He turned away from me then and stared at the water. He didn't say a word. He was deep in thought. And as I stood there with him, I realized that he was tuning me out...lost in his own thoughts. I might as well have been alone, I thought sadly.

And with that revelation, there was only one thing left to say. "Take me home."

13

As I rode back to my place, I did my best to memorize the feel of his body pressed into mine. I held back tears as I knew I had done the right thing, but it had been hard, oh so hard. I didn't understand why he couldn't just love me like I loved him. He was a good man. I couldn't deny that. But he kept me at arm's length...he clearly never wanted my love.

I had complicated things by developing feelings for him. All the pain I felt was technically my fault, but falling for him had never been my plan. It had never been my plan to fall in love. But life was funny like that.

He pulled up in front of my apartment and I promptly jumped off without his assistance. Nothing more needed to be said and he didn't look at me anyway. As soon as I was off his motorcycle, he started his bike and drove off without a backward glance. He hadn't even looked at me.

Feeling defeated, I walked up to my apartment and went in. I was emotionally exhausted and I thought to myself yet again how I had terrible taste in men.

It was funny though because, of course, life had a funny way of mixing things up. The moment I realized that I could stand on my own and just be me also happened to be the moment that I realized that I was in love.

I put my feet up on the couch and was determined to just go to sleep there when a knock sounded at my door.

I knew who it was before I even opened the door.

"Hi," he said, simply standing there still looking perturbed. "Can I come in?"

"We're done, Erik."

"Please, I just want two minutes...if you don't want to hear what I have to say then feel free to kick me out."

"No. I don't want to hear anything you have to say."

"I want to tell you." He paused and said with a sigh, "I want to tell you about Shana."

"Shana?"

"My ex-wife."

All plans of taking a nap on the couch faded as I moved to let him cross the entrance. I closed and locked the door, gestured for him to sit down and then sat in the loveseat across from him and said, "Alright, go."

He sat down heavily on the couch and brought his eyes up to mine. "We were high school sweethearts. We met when we were both 14."

"Let me guess. She was beautiful, a cheerleader maybe?"

He laughed. "She was beautiful to me. She wore really dark lipstick and eyeliner. Totally goth."

My eyebrows shot up in surprise.

"She was really into Alice Cooper and Black Sabbath."

"Wow, I wouldn't have expected that."

He shrugged. "I liked her. I followed her around most of the time. Sort of like a puppy. She finally noticed me when we were sophomores. I felt it was the luckiest day of my life when she said hi to me. But I was always getting in trouble in school and her parents didn't think I was good enough for their daughter. And they were right at first." He shrugged sheepishly. "I wasn't. But she was loyal. She stayed with me. She went off to college and I started working construction jobs. She even married me after she graduated."

"You sound surprised."

"Shana could have had any man she wanted and yet she chose me. I thought I was special."

When he didn't continue, I prompted him with, "And then what happened?"

He shrugged. "We were happily married for about five years. At least, I thought we were happily married."

He got up and went to look out of my window. The view from my window was only the parking lot. I knew he wasn't seeing the view in front of him, he was just staring into a void, thinking of his past. "I came home early from a job that had gotten rained out and I saw a car in front of our apartment. I didn't think much of it. It was a big complex, visitors came and went all the time. I walked upstairs and I could hear them from the living room as soon as I stepped through the door."

My heart hurt for him. "Did you confront them?"

"I needed proof...so I made myself walk in. I was just going to turn around and walk away. But I made my legs walk toward our bedroom. I pushed the door open and saw them going at it."

He folded his arms across his chest and crossed his legs at the ankles. "A few seconds later they noticed me standing there. The guy screwing her jumped up and scrambled off of her when he spotted me. I didn't recognize him and didn't even bother to stop him. All I could see was her. He was barely a blimp on my radar. He was no one to me, but she was everything. My world."

I didn't dare interrupt.

"So, after that, I threw myself into my work. Got my contractor's license. I started flipping houses. I started acquiring more real estate. I made several good investments. Started my own company. I was so driven. Driven to prove her wrong."

"Prove her wrong?" I didn't quite understand.

"She blamed me for her cheating. She said that she was unhappy...that she deserved more than what some high-school graduate could give her."

"I'm so sorry, Erik."

He shrugged. "I felt emasculated. I'm not going to lie. I thought I was doing all I could to provide a good life for my wife and when she unceremoniously told me that I wasn't, I just felt like a failure. And I blamed myself. I definitely blamed myself. I said to myself, if only I had made more money, been able to give her more things, took her on fancy trips, she would have been happy."

"As someone who was cheated on, I get it, but she made a decision to cheat instead of leave. If she was unhappy, she should have just left."

He shrugged. "I figured she would have eventually, she just needed a way out. I knew after she had graduated from college that we had grown apart, but I was still holding on to that memory of that person I had known and loved when I was 14."

"Did you ever find out who the guy was that she was sleeping with?"

He nodded. "Turned out the guy she was sleeping with was her boss. She married him later. I heard they have a few kids together."

"Doesn't it suck when your ex isn't miserable without you?"

He laughed. "Yeah. I was sort of hoping a sink hole would come and swallow her up, but no such luck."

"Yeah, I secretly hoped Wyatt's special parts would fall off."

Erik grimaced. "Yikes."

I giggled and he sat down next to me. "So, we both were cheated on."

"Yep."

"For some reason, your story seems worse. More of a betrayal."

"I don't know...I guess in some ways. But I made a mistake in marrying the person I thought I knew instead of the person she actually was."

"I understand that. I married Wyatt because I thought I should. I thought I was proving something to my mom and dad, like, 'Look, Mom and Dad, I did it without you guys. I graduated from college, I'm marrying an engineer. You not loving me didn't faze me! I'm successful. I even have my own company.'" I shook my head, regretting my past decisions, but understanding that they made me who I was.

"You lived your life for someone else, when you really thought you were thumbing your nose at them. I get it. I became a billionaire to impress my ex who cheated on me and it got me nowhere. I'm struggling to start a family and she already has one. Money didn't bring her back to me or give me the family I wanted."

"Same here," I said with a sigh. "I thought I was building a future, stability. And instead I ended up broke, alone and kind of, sort of homeless."

"We're quite a pair, aren't we?"

"We're dysfunctional and I'm tired of being dysfunctional. I want to be a little selfish for a change and just focus on what makes me happy instead of trying to impress or prove something to others."

He smiled. "I don't think it's selfish to live for yourself instead of others."

I thought about that. Maybe that's what Uncle Niko had been trying to share with me all along.

Erik reached for my chin then and tilted my face up to meet his. "What do you say, Misha? Would you like to be selfish with me? And just be with each other because that's what we want and not because it's what's expected?"

"How romantic," I said sarcastically, as I wrapped my arms around his neck.

"Or you can just be with me because you love me and I love you." He pressed his forehead against mine.

My heart skipped a beat at his words. "Uh oh, Erik… you told me that you love me. Do you think the earth will stop spinning on its axis in shock?"

"Hold on, let's see." He paused theatrically and then said, "I think we'll be okay. No need to notify NASA."

"You're so romantic," I teased.

He shrugged. "Romance is what I know."

"You're kind of good at it."

"I'm good at a lot of things…but I'll be especially good at loving you."

"Delilah," I called once, waiting for a reply. "Lilah!" I tried again. No answer.

Erik walked in at that moment covered in rain with Jonas on his back. Lilah and Jonas were our foster children, and eventually if everything went right in court in a few weeks they would become ours forever. They had become my world and frankly, I couldn't imagine life now without them.

Delilah finally made an appearance in the kitchen. She had a pair of scissors in her hand and was carrying a doll.

"Scissors, Lilah," I said sternly and placed my hand out and waited for her to turn them over to me. "You know you're not allowed to have scissors," I said for good measure.

She pouted but did as she was told. She was two, going on three, and she was quite a handful. We'd been her foster parents since she was one and it was shocking to me how much she had grown and how much a part of me she was.

Jonas had joined our family a year ago. He was seven, going on eight and had a few developmental issues that mostly affected his speech patterns. His speech was improving greatly, I thought. His speech pathologist was worth her weight in gold.

Shortly after Erik and I had married, we had decided to become foster parents. And we couldn't have been happier with our decision. Erik seemed to glow in their presence. Being a father suited him. But I wasn't surprised, I always knew it would.

"Hey, beautiful," he said, kissing me as he sat Jonas down. Jonas immediately went running after the dog we'd inherited. We had found the dog after a particularly devastating tropical storm, running across the street, dodging cars covered in dirt and shaking. We had added him to our family and the kids, for whatever reason, named him Robot.

I heard a loud bang and then a crash. And then laughter.

"They're tearing our house apart," I said and then yelled, "Are you guys okay in there?"

Jonas called back, "Robot knocked over your vase."

"I told you to get rid of that vase," Erik said, shaking his head and rummaging through the refrigerator.

"But it goes so well with the room."

"If Robot knocks it over again, it's going to go so well in the garbage."

"Ouch...that hurt...you're killing me here."

"Sacrifices must be made for the sake of the family."

"And what have you sacrificed?" I said, putting my hand on my hip and trying not to smile.

"My hair. It's going gray around my beard."

I leaned forward and looked really hard. There was exactly one gray hair. I told him that and he looked relieved.

"You're so vain."

"I am. That is true. But that's what you love about me. I stay looking good for you."

"Yes...that's one of the things I love about you, for sure. You're still hot."

"Of course, there are like 100 more things you love about me, but we don't have time to hear them all so you can start with your top 20."

I rolled my eyes. "Hon, on a good day, I can probably come up with a solid two, maybe three reasons that I love you."

"Harsh."

"The truth always is," I teased.

The doorbell rang then and I opened it up to see Oliver standing there.

Jonas and Lilah came running to the door and plowed into him. Each one hugged one of his bony legs and I didn't know how he didn't topple over.

"Grandpa O!" they shouted in happiness. That's what he told them to call him. He thought it sounded cool.

"How are my little buddies doing?" he said, trying to pick them both up at the same time. Somehow he managed, but at one point I thought they were all going to hit the floor.

"You're just in time for dinner," I said.

He looked happily at the kids and then to me. "I knew it. I knew you and Erik would be perfect for each other. All your happiness is due to my meddling." He looked so smug.

"Well, now every single person you know is paired up, so you can stop trying to set everyone up and focus on yourself."

He looked shocked by the idea. "You mean dating? Ha! No, thank you. No way."

I raised a brow, and he chuckled and walked away chatting happily with the kids when the doorbell rang again.

"Simon got lost on the way here, so that's why I'm late. How did he get lost? I don't know. It's the only house on the island," my grandmother said as she came in. "He's still in the car talking to some girl on the phone. He said she's his girlfriend. I told him that he's too young to commit to one woman. I told him that I'm dating at least three people right now. Keeps life interesting."

I didn't know how to respond to that, so I smartly said nothing.

"Where are my grandkids?" she asked, looking around.

"With our guest," I said cryptically.

"Hey, Oliver, come here for a second...I want you to meet someone."

Oliver came into the room and smiled at my granny. She smiled back and seemed to stick her chest out. I held in a laugh.

"Grandma, this is Oliver. Oliver, this is Grandma. Umm, I mean, I call her Grandma because she's my grandma, but you can call her--."

"Katherine," she said, practically purring at him and offering her hand. "But my friends call me Kat."

Oliver took my grandmother's hand and kissed the back of it. "Kat, it is a pleasure to meet you. Can I escort you to the dinner table?"

"Play your cards right and you'll get to do a lot more than that," she said flirtatiously and I blushed.

Oliver was less of a prude than me. He laughed, offered his arm and she took it. They walked away together with their heads toward each other giggling over a shared joke that I was sure I didn't want to hear.

Erik walked toward me then and said, "So the matchmaker has met his match, huh?"

"Frankly, she's probably more than he can handle, but what the hell, he might as well try, right?"

"You were more than I could handle and look how that turned out."

"Yeah, you lucked out."

"I thank my lucky stars every day."

"As well you should," I said, hugging his neck. He lowered his face toward my own and said, "Thanks for loving me...because I wholeheartedly, unequivocally love you."

I smiled up at him and said teasingly, "Your use of big words is so sexy."

He laughed and said, "And an 'I love you too' would have sufficed."

"I love you too," I kissed him slowly, appreciating the seconds we had to exchange that kiss since alone time was rare nowadays with two kids underfoot.

And just as predicted, when we broke from the kiss, two pairs of eyes were staring at us.

Jonas looked ill. "Gross," he said. And Lilah looked unperturbed. She held up a sippy cup and hit me with it. "Juice, Mommy."

"Duty calls." And with that, I tossed an arm around

Jonas's shoulder and took Lilah's hand. And as I turned the corner I looked back at Erik who looked at us lovingly. I smiled and he smiled back.

I knew exactly who I was now. I wasn't just Erik's wife or Jonas's and Delilah's soon to be "real" mom. I was Misha. A re-married divorcee. A failed business owner making a comeback. A foster mom. A wife. A friend. I was all those things, but they didn't solely define me because most importantly, I was loved.

DARK DESIRES
~ A billionaire dark romance series ~
Dark Desire
Dark Rules
Dark Secret
Dark Time
Dark Truth

BARRE TO BAR
~ A billionaire second chance series ~
Dancing With Lies
Dancing With Temptation
Dancing With Doubt
Dancing With Guilt
Dancing With Redemption

TWISTED INTENTION
~ A billionaire revenge romance series ~
Twisted Beauty
Twisted Love
Twisted Fate

Mafia's Obsession
~ A hot mafia romance series ~
Mafia's Dirty Secret
Mafia's Fake Bride
Mafia's Final Play

Screaming Demons
~ An MC romance series full of suspense ~
Rough Start
Rough Ride
Rough Choice
Rough Patch
Rough Return
Rough Road
Rough Trip
Rough Night
Rough Love

Standalone Contemporary Romance
Billionaire in Vegas
Billionaire Hunt

Billionaire's Game
Billionaire Retreat
Billionaire On Air
A Chance To Love
Somebody To Love
Not Mine To Love

Check out Summer's entire collection at
www.summercooper.com/books

ABOUT SUMMER COOPER

Thank you so much for reading. Without you, it wouldn't be possible for me to be a full-time author. I hope you enjoy reading my books as much as I do writing them.

Besides (obviously!) reading and writing, I also love cuddling my dogs, shouting at Alexa, being upside down (aka Yoga) and driving my family cray-cray!

Get in touch at
hello@summercooper.com
www.summercooper.com

facebook.com/summercooperauthor
instagram.com/summercooperauthor
goodreads.com/summercooper
bookbub.com/profile/summer-cooper